ISBN: 0692423273
ISBN-13: 9780692423271
Library of Congress Control Number: 2015905806
Createspace Independent Publishing Platform, North Charleston, SC

Time Trip

Alice Frost origins

Written By

Jace Watkins

The ships construction had been completed for a year

Now it was in orbit waiting for its crew the five men and women given

The mission exploring the new planet Gemini 1 which had just been

Discovered readings show that the planet is habitable of sustain life

The journey was going to be somewhat instantious, the ships engine was

A prototype basically how it works is every point in space has a number

The computer aligned with the engine, picks out that number you put in.

The engine basically teleports the ship to the coridents in the computer.

The ship has state of the art planetary travel controls.

The mission to study investigate and determine if the planet is suitable for

Colonization. The ship was massive the size of the Pyramids

Construction begin in 2045 with it taking 12 years to finish.

It was mostly automated with robots that's why such a small crew

The AI on the ship were a12s they looked and acted like humans

This was the first mission that these a12s were going to be used

They would handle most of the labor that would occur on the mission

These a12s were different from other humanoid Als these had human brains

Where the others uses CPU there are 4000 of these a12s on the ship.

.The crew was on earth's largest space station

About to board to take the shuttle to the ship the Explorer. Commander

Alice Frost the last to get into her seat. She was an Intelligent young

Twenty Seven year old American, she was in charge of the mission

Next In Command Was Dry John Den ware he was the ship's doctor. He was the eldest

Member at 62 he had been in the air force for 30 years and he had been with

This project since it started Astronought Chase Hopkins was in charge of the

Ships life supports.   He was a tall slender 34 year old American he was a

Bit of a joker. Ashley Hartford was assigned to this mission for her ability

To get things done she was one tough marine she has went into many suicide

Missions and came out of it with no problems she's the insurance policy on

This mission. Private Jason Lane got assigned to this mission last year

He has been prepping ever since. He was soft spoken and shy. His duties

Included keeping repairs on the a12s.Last was science engineer Katie Peterson

She was there to study the local wildlife and inhabits should there be any

On the planet. Once there they intend on setting up a base on the planet and

And leaving behind two thousand of the a12s. The ship was built to split

Into two different ships in orbit around the planet, one stays in orbit as

A space station aliening itself with the ground base the other half returns

To earth with the crew. That was the plan. "Captain Frost we're docking

With the ship now" The pilot of the shuttle said. All right people make

Sure you don't leave anything behind "Hey commander I sure hope you can fly that

Thing". "You do your job Mr. Hopkins I'll Do Mine". "Yes Commander". The crew steps into

The elevator and the door closes. "All right everybody this is it when the door

Opens go to your post, we're going halfway across the universe in a blink of

An eye so the quicker we go the faster we get to Gemini"." I can't wait to see

It I mean think about it another earth like planet and it's in the oldest part

Of the universe so who knows what's going to be on the planet" "Don't get your

Hopes up Miss Preston could turn out to be a dust ball."Yeah I Know captain

But I just know the info is good. "And this info written millions of years ago

A lot can happen in millions of years look what happened to the dinosaurs"

"I Know Captain but I'm here to study it" "Ok people lets go". The doors of the

Elevator open and the crew steps out and each go to the post they have

Trained for. In the control room The Commander and Hopkins have prepped for

Launch. "Hopkins put the coridents in the computer". "Yes Commander" The ship floats

Silently in space around the earth. "Hit the Juice Hopkins". The ship

Disappears into nothing its current location in orbit around Gemini 1

Deep space the planet Gemini 1, the planet is a blue life giver its beauty

Matches earth and as you would turn a light bulb on so does the ship

The explorer pops on in orbit just as if you would turn a light on.

The technology in this ship is unbelievable and it was acquired in a

Information exchange from our friends from the stars. The crew along with

The a12s get on with their duties. A hall way long and wide. Three a12s

Are walking down it, one stops at a doorway. He enters carrying a devise

In his hand. He scans some hardware inside of the lab where miss Peterson

Is working. She needs to stay focused at the eight monitors an array of

Instruments delivering data from the planet. She finds what she expects

Breathable air, H2o, land masses. She walks to the port view window she

Marvels at Gemini. The port window was huge, from here Miss Peterson had

Literally a two trillion dollar view. She sees that there was three moons and

Stars that she has never saw before. The a12 turns and walks out the door

Miss Preston comes back to her monitors. She turns some knobs types some

Information in the computer. She speaks out loud. "This cannot be, if this

Data is correct we have made a time jump one hundred million years into the

Past and the data does not lie". "Someone really messed this up". Peterson

Goes to her intercom. "Commander Frost we have a problem I need you
down here

Immediately". "Roger Preston I'll be right there". Commander Frost starts to

Get out of her chair. "MR. Hopkins stay in this orbit it's on autopilot so

You should be just fine". "Yes Commander". She walks down the hallway heading

Toward the science lab.A12s walking back and fourth

The A12s consisted of both male and female. They basically are experiments

Combining AI with human lifestyles. The A12s have everything a human has except for

Internal organs except for their brains which was soldiers that was killed

In combat. The technology was there to try this experiment so they saved has

Many as they could. The Captain walks into the lab room and walks over to

Preston."Ok what's the problem"? "Commander my readings on the system array

Is giving information that we have actually traveled to the past 100 million

Years". The captains face showed an almost turmoil of fear." I was afraid of this. In

One of my briefings my commanding officer said this could happen". "What do we?

Do captain". "As of right now Miss Preston we are stranded here the jump in time

Has most definitely damaged the engine and unaligned the point of reference

One which we need to get back home. "This may just be our home now here on Gemini"

"There's got to be another way commander". "Miss Preston the guys at Nasa was still

Working on this error scenario we would be like cave men trying to turn on

A TV all we can do is put the a12s on the engine and hope they can find

A solution it was supposed to be a 1 in a million that this could happen

So we weren't trained for this, if the planet is livable we should be ok

We have a work force, we have technology we may live our lives out here".

"Miss Preston go get the doctor and meet in the control room we will inform

The others". "Yes Commander". "A12f go activate the rest of the a12's"."Yes

Captain". Back in the control room the crew are about to be told the news.

Last to enter the control room was Lane. It was a large room that was

Similar to an office with a lot of high Tec devices."Ok people we have had

A major system failure we have traveled one hundred million years in the
past

Our engine has suffered a critical failure and if we could get it to work

We don't know if it will be one hundred million years in the past on earth

If we made it back". "Commander how could this happen". "Well private Lane

The engine had a failure during our instantious travel in the middle of it

While we were nowhere in space the engine stopped for a second threes

Three things that happens when this occurs, 1 you go forward in time 2 you

Go backward in time, 3 you blow up, this is a one in a million occurrence".

DR. Den ware sees the terra building up on the crews face. "Everybody remain

Calm we have supply's we have medical aid I'm your doctor we have weapons we are

Going to be ok"."Everyone listen all of you suite up we'll be taking a ship

Down to the planet for observation a12a you oversee the repairs on the

Engine". "Yes Commander". "Load up people we don't know what's down there"

"What do we bring Commander"? "Bring everything". The crew heads to the weapon

Room and suits up with every devise that they can carry. They head for the

Hanger. They step to the door Dr. Den ware placed his thumb on the pad. The

Door disappeared into thin air right in front of them. The crew steps

Through the door into the hanger bay. Ships of all shapes and sizes are

Lined all the way down the hanger bay. "Commander Can you fly all of these?"

"Yeah most I have flown Miss Preston". "So how many can the a12s fly?"

"They can fly them all ". The crew and 7 a12s get into a large ship with

Windows in the front as wide as a house. Its shape was bullet design it's fully

Loaded with all the bells and Whistles. Hopkins sits in the copilot chair he

Buckles himself into his chair. He begins to prep the ship for launch.

The commander sits in the pilots chair and buckles in.She starts with her prep

For takeoff. Seconds later the ship rises slowly and silently. A voice comes

On the intercom. "Docking bay air lock in 3 2 1 lock". The doors in the hanger

Disappears into nothing and you see space with all its beauty. You could fit

200 of the old airlines through the hanger. The ship rises about 20 more feet from

All other ships that are still on the ground. The ship floats out the air lock doors

And into space. Even though the ship that the crew is in right now is big it still

Looks like a grape sitting next to a watermelon. "Everybody's stay on your radio

If we get separated". "Yes captain.". The ship floated about 60 meters from the

Main ship. "Commander ready for launch". "Roger Hopkins firing main engines in 3 2 1 fire"

The commander uses the ships pc in plug in her brain so she uses her hands to fly

It but also her mind.

The ships propulsion system is electrometric it's electrical. The ships well design shows

As it enters the atmosphere. There's no drag on the ship as it glides through the

Fall. They Level up and hover about twenty thousand feet. The commander looks at her

Monitor. "I'm picking up life signs changing course". The ship takes off at a high rate

Of speed the crew members are all buckled in but they have a very good view.

They came down over water they have not made land yet. They are flying about 300

Feet from the surface of the water."Ok people get ready we're fixing to hit the jump

5 4 3 2 1 jump". The ship disappears leaving a trailing fiery tale in the sky.

The ship reappears 700 miles ahead. "Commander we are approaching a land mass"

"Roger Hopkins hit the boosters" "hitting the juice commander".

Moments later. "Commander I'm picking up a large group of life signs just up ahead

"Hopkins zero in on the signal". Yes sir. It's just to the north commander we should

Be seeing it any second". As the ship begins to slow they approach what we would

Call a medieval castle it looks ancient. The ship is about 300 feet off the

Ground. "Commander I see people". "I'm lowering the ship I see one in the forest

We need a test subject, Mr. Hopkins throw the beam on him and zip him on board"

Hopkins hits a switch and a large beam of light comes on the native and

Immobilizes him .Hopkins hits another button and the native blinks out of sight

"Ok captain I have him he is in cell 3". "A12 bring me this native". "Yes commander"

"We have to find a place to set the ship down so it's out of sight". The commander flies

To the south of the castle and lands the ship in a medow.The captain gets out of

Her chair. The doors open in the control room. The A12 walks the native toward the

Captain. The man looks freighted he is wearing old rags. He looks very much like

Our ancestors there was nothing special about this man."What's he saying commander".

"I Don't Know Hopkins". "A12 see if you can find this language in your data

Base". "Yes captain".   The Man keeps talking confused and frightened.

"Commander I Have a Match these people are descendants of the alien race Quad rends

This race was destroyed over 150 million years ago this must have been

One of their colony's that they was involved with before they got hit".

"A12 what's he saying". "Commander he says what country are you from".

"Tell him we are from the stars and we mean him no harm". The A12 translates.

"Captain he wants to know if we are GODS". "Yes tell him we are GODS and he

Must do what we say". "Commander he says yes he will". "Now ask him whose castle that

Is". The A12 translates in the alien language. "Commander he said it was built by

His ancestors to guard against something we would call a wolf". "A12 ask him

Is the ruler violent"? "He says no commander." "Put him back in cell 3 A12".

"Yes Commander". "Ok everybody head for the weapons room we are going in the dark"

 In the weapons room they each suit up with every advantage they could come

Across, mag belts, taticital gear. The five head out of the equipment room fully

Stocked. They go to the docking bay doors and push the thumb pad. The doors dissolves

Into nothing they walk out of the ship and down the ramp the door pops back

Into being they step off the ramp."Ok keep your guard up if you get in trouble

Hit the power on your mag belt and get 50 feet up out of danger everybody clear"

"Roger" "clear" "yes sir". The party consist of five crew and 5 A12s. They start

Walking toward the castle which is about 300 yards north. The A12s see in the dark

But the crew does not so they move slower. The A12s are carrying fully auto cannons

And the crew has lighter light weapons. They move slowly through the forest

Very similar to earths forest. Strangely something sounding a lot like a wolf

Begins to howl off in the distance ironically the system has three moons and

There all full tonight. The A12s spot something. They bring their weapons up

"Captain you and the others have to leave there's hostile animals out in the

Distance"."A12b and A12c stay here and guard our rear, the rest of you to

The castle". They get about 150 feet away and they hear the two A12s firing

There auto cannons 5, 10 seconds maybe and then there was nothing. The rest of

The group reach the castle."Ok everybody hit the power on your mag belt and go

Over the wall". The five humans and three A12s rise up silently as if riding

On the wind they float gently with a few adjustments on the mag belt they begin

To move forward and lower back to the ground. The castle looked to be ancient

It was huge .There was statues looking similar to a wolf. "Look around everybody

Hopkins check those doors". "It's sealed from the inside captain" "ok people

Looks like everyone is asleep we come back first light". The group goes back

Over the wall. They come along what's left of the two A12s ripped to pieces

In a dozen pieces. "Be on your guard everyone A12s scanners on". "Yes sir"

The group pushes on slowly. "There's the ship". "Hold on Hopkins lets send one of

The A12s across the field first". "A12d move to the ship". "Yes commander".

The A12 Walks out from the wood line cannon and scanner ready .He makes it

To the ship."OK Everybody move toward the ship. The group gets half way across

The meow 50 feet from the ship and a giant monster jumps them. Growling showing

Its teeth. This is what ripped the other 2 a12s apart .Captian frost raises her

Weapon toward the creature she fires once. A brilliant blue light emerges from her

Weapon striking the creature which was standing on two legs. The powerful weapon

Is a prototype given to the young commander .It takes the creature down .It

Does not move. The group hover over the dead animal."Somethings happening

Commander ". They all looked on as the dead creature turns before their eyes into

A dead man. "Ok that was creepy was this creature a human or an animal". "I'm not

Sure Miss Preston". "Dr. Do you have any input". "Commander It could be a virus, we

Should bring it aboard and do some test".

Back on board the ship now. The A12s have brought the body on board. It lays in

The lab where Katie Preston is examining the body. She finds what one would find

In a dead body minus the burnt energy blast mark on its chest.

She's waiting for a blood test to finish up

And give her report to the commander back in the control room.

Commander Frost and the others talk. "We're in over our head here Commander this is

A hostile planet if there's one there's more, the other guy we picked up is probably

One too we should get out of here while we can". "Hopkins we're not leaving

Until we talk to who lives behind those walls we put the test subject in

A holding cell and go to the temple first light". "A12 go put the test subject

In cell 1a" "Yes Commander". In the lab miss Peterson, Heartford, and an a12 talk

With the test subject while Miss Preston draws some blood. A Buzzer goes off. "That's

The blood test for the dead guy let's see". Miss Preston Looks at the blood sample

Under a microscope now with the data on screen."Yeah this guy is defently infected

Hartford". Hartford never said much she she stood shaking her head. "It's some

Kind of blood disorder". An A12 comes in the door. "My orders are to put the

Test subject in a holding cell". "Ok I'm done with him just be careful with his

Leg he had a wound when the a12 translated all we could make out was animal bit

I patched him up". "Yes sir". The a12 takes the man out of the room and down

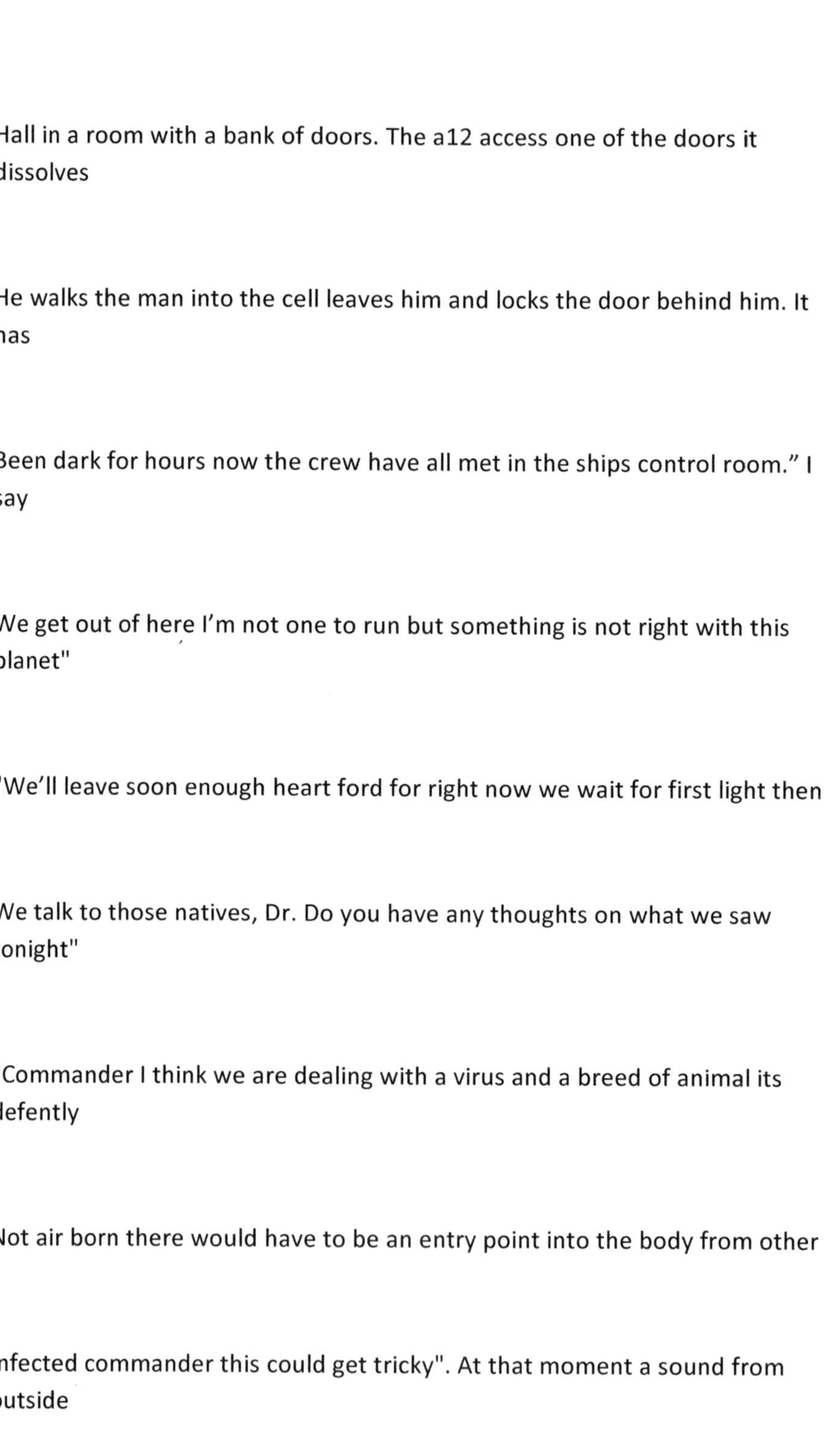

Hall in a room with a bank of doors. The a12 access one of the doors it dissolves

He walks the man into the cell leaves him and locks the door behind him. It has

Been dark for hours now the crew have all met in the ships control room." I say

We get out of here I'm not one to run but something is not right with this planet"

"We'll leave soon enough heart ford for right now we wait for first light then

We talk to those natives, Dr. Do you have any thoughts on what we saw tonight"

"Commander I think we are dealing with a virus and a breed of animal its defently

Not air born there would have to be an entry point into the body from other

Infected commander this could get tricky". At that moment a sound from outside

The ship things moving and growling in all directions." Mr. Hopkins hit

The flood lights on the exterior" Hopkins walks to the control switch board and

Presses a button. Lights come on the outside of the ship. All the crew stare out

The port main window and see thousands of these creatures that attacked them

 Earlier .They was just outside the glass. The Commander's heart skipped a beat

She just realized if they felt we was here they might come through the glass

"Mr. HOPKINS HIT THE BLAST SHEILD WINDOWS!!" Three feet thick shield doors

Slowly drops down. One of the creatures spot it moving .The creature springs to the

Ship bringing many of the other creatures with it. They start to pound on the dropping

Shield doors missing the glass by inches. The crew gets a close up view of the

Creatures one pounding at the shield door while another howls in the background.

The shield windows are down fully now but the crew can still hear the creatures

 Outside." Mr. Hopkins hit the video link from outside". "Right commander".

The video comes on the main screen with the same picture as they saw before the

The blast windows came up. "Commander now I understand why the doors on the temple

Was sealed from the inside"." I think you are right Dr.".ize"Mr. Hopkins lock down the

Ship nothing gets in or out"."Dr. Let's take a trip to the lab everyone else

Be on alert and under no circumstance open any hatch door keep your personal weapon

On hand". "Lane take a a12 and watch the test subject" "Yes captain"

Private Lane and an a12 walk down a hallway other a12 passes by them. Private

Lane feels uneasy after seeing what he saw outside he knows what they're dealing

With he does not care what the doctor says it's no virus one word comes to his

Mind over and over, werewolf he thinks to himself. He looks over to the A12

As they are walking to the holding cell."A12 take this it's getting dangerous around

Here". He hands the A12 a high energy light pistol similar to the one the

Captain uses. "Yes sir what is the target?" "Anything not one of us". "Yes sir"

They walk to the room with the bank of doors. Private Lane looks through the cell

He sees the man sitting on the bed. The man sees Lane watching him. The man

Stands up and walks to the door he is saying something but the private does not

Understand him. "what's he saying A12"."He said he would like something to eat"

What do you think A12 can we open the doors." "He does not seem violent sir"

"Ok I'm going to open the door watch him A12" "yes sir". Lane pushes in the

Numbers to open the door it dissolves into nothing. Private Lane motions

The man to come out he walks him to the table in the middle of the room.

The man sits down."A12 bring me two meal rations from the locker in the corner"

"Yes sir". The a12 brought to the table two plastic bags that have ready made

Food. When It is opened it has a reaction to the air and the food forms and

Cooks. Private Lane slides out the plate from the bag and puts the plate

In front of the man. He starts to smell of the food he dives into the food like

A starving man would using both hands to eat. He eats both meal rations. The a12

And Private Lane stand up from the table. They motion for the man to get up

"A12 ask him what his name is" "Yes sir". "He said his name is Rollo Sir".

They start to walk him back in the cell but before they get to the cell

Rollo Bends over in pain grabbing his stomach screaming in pain. He falls to his

Knees."A12 go get the captain and the Dr." The a12 runs out of the room down

The hall into a maze of halls. But the A12 knows where he is at. He calculates

It will take 8 mins to reach the lab. The doctor and the Commander and Miss

Preston

Are all talking about the blood taken from the test subject. Preston ask the Dr.

To take a look. The Dr. Looks at the blood mutating in front of his eyes. "Yes he

Is infected" "Are you sure Dr." "100 percent sure captain" "Dr. We need

Need to get that man off the ship" "I Believe your right Commander". At that

Moment the A12 arrives. "Sir Private Lane needs you at the holding cell

There's something wrong with the test subject. "Dr. He is mutating keep your

Weapons ready". "Yes commander we are with you" The three crew members and

Two a12s walk the halls that lead to the holding cell. Back in with private lane

Rollo lays on the floor shaking uncontrollably. The first thing that pops in

Private Lanes head is he is having an allergic reaction to the food. But then the

Private saw what was about to take place .Rollo starts to grow hair his finger

Nails grow instantly. His screams was different now with a deeper voice and

In an instant Rollo is fully transformed. He jumps at incredible speed and kills

Private Lane with one blow to the head. The creature howls while standing over

The body of private lane. The creature hears the other crew members coming

Down the hall. He looks at all of his surroundings. The only way out

Is through the door or up into the air shaft. He goes up rips open the air shaft

And jumps invite was a perfect fit for him he barely had to walk on all fours.

The creature came out of the air shaft half way across the ship. He stands

In the hall smelling in different directions he comes to a door its set

On automatic open so when the creature steps in front of it the door opens.

As the creature stepped in the room he instantly spotted Chase Hopkins his back

To the creature. They was about 30 feet apart. Hopkins hears the wolf breathing

But Hopkins stays motionless. Slowly he reaches for his light pistol on his belt

The creature leaps at him. Hopkins turns and fires two shots of brilliant

Light balls that strike the creature in the head, but the creature is moving

So fast its dead body keeps coming toward Hopkins. It lands right on Hopkins.

He blocks the impact with his hand but the creatures claws stab Hopkins in

The chest but Hopkins in unharmed other than that. Just a scratch he tells himself

The creature transforms back to human form right in front of Hopkins. "What the

Hell are you Pal".

Hopkins stood over the dead body wondering if anybody was hurt during this

Man's escape. "Computer" Yes sir the computer said in a women's voice. "Patch me

Through to the commander ""Yes sir line patched sir" "Commander"." Mr. Hopkins I was

Just going to call you our test subject has killed private lane and escaped"

 "Well he didn't escape I Just shot him" "How bad was the attack captain"

"The doctor said his neck had been broken" "Dam" "Hopkins was you injured"

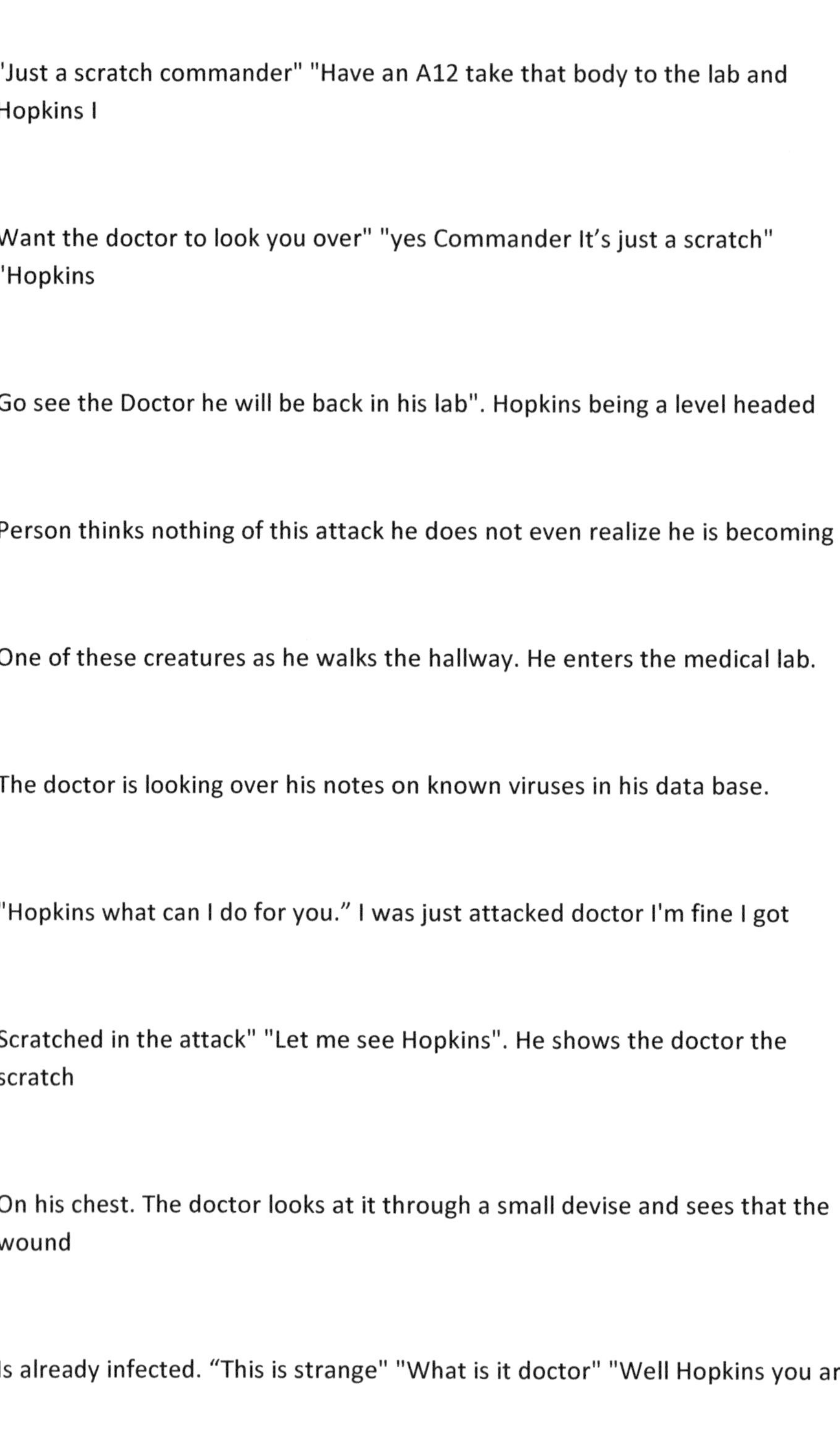

"Just a scratch commander" "Have an A12 take that body to the lab and Hopkins I

Want the doctor to look you over" "yes Commander It's just a scratch" "Hopkins

Go see the Doctor he will be back in his lab". Hopkins being a level headed

Person thinks nothing of this attack he does not even realize he is becoming

One of these creatures as he walks the hallway. He enters the medical lab.

The doctor is looking over his notes on known viruses in his data base.

"Hopkins what can I do for you." I was just attacked doctor I'm fine I got

Scratched in the attack" "Let me see Hopkins". He shows the doctor the scratch

On his chest. The doctor looks at it through a small devise and sees that the wound

Is already infected. "This is strange" "What is it doctor" "Well Hopkins you are

Infected with whatever virus that creature was carrying I don't know what the

Affect will be on your body but I'm recommending that you be quarantined and we

Leave this planet as soon as we can". "I feel fine doc" "Your infected Hopkins

The best thing we can do for you is try to get back to earth fast" "A12 escort

Mr. Hopkins to a holding cell and report back to me when you are done" Yes Doctor"

The A12 and Hopkins walk out of the medical lab and down the hall. The doctor

Hails for the Commander over the computer."   Commander ""Yes Doctor" "Hopkins has been

Infected I'm not sure the effects that will be taking place on his body but

I had him put in a holding cell" "Doctor what are your thoughts on all of this

"I think we should leave this planet captain as soon as we can". "Yes I agree

Doctor this mission is over I will inform the others". The captain patches

The ships intercom and informs the crew that's left to come to the control room.

Peterson and Hartford hear the captain and drop what they are doing and head

For the control room. On the way there they all pass Hopkins and the A12.

"Hopkins you are going the wrong way did you not hear the captain". Hopkins

Stands staring at the rest of the crew not knowing what to say. "Hopkins what's

Wrong with you" Preston ask. They all stand for a few seconds not saying

Anything. Hopkins starts to speak but before he can open his mouth he feels

An intense pain in his stomach. He bends over in pain falling to his knees.

The crew and the A12 reach to help Hopkins up. In a matter of five seconds Hopkins

Transforms Into the wolf. He rises to his feet now out of his clothes fully

Transformed teeth sharp as razors. He had growled a full 3 feet in height now

Standing seven and a half feet tall. With one swipe he takes the A12s head

Clean off it falls to the ground lifeless. He goes for Peterson and does the

Same to her. Heartford pulls her weapon but the wolf is on her and rips her to

Pieces. In A matter of seconds the entire party are dead. The wolf stands over

The dead and howls with its razor sharp teeth dripping with blood. Another A12

Come around the corner and see what has happened. The wolf turns and on all

Four runs down the other way escaping into the air vents. The A12 is not even

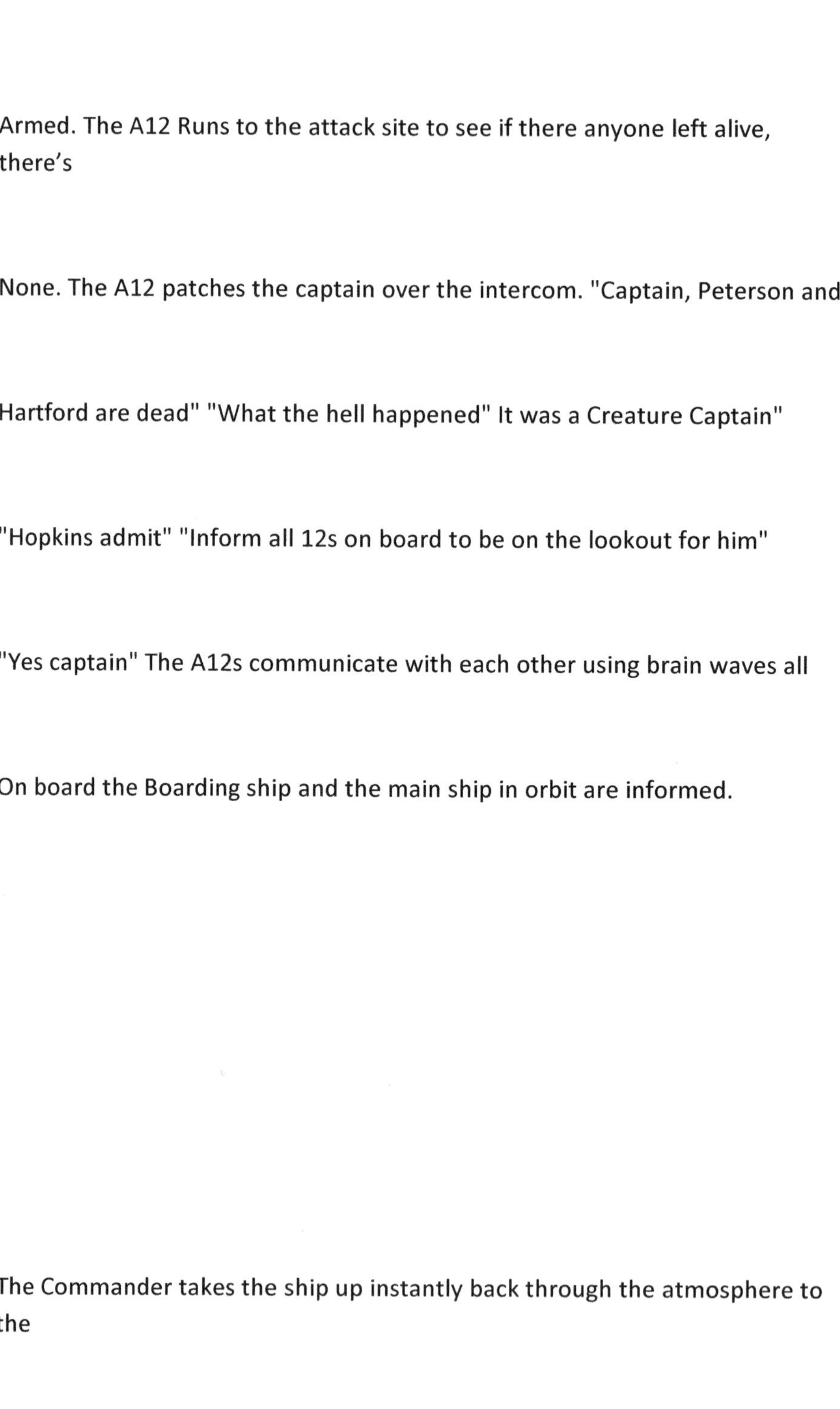

Armed. The A12 Runs to the attack site to see if there anyone left alive, there's

None. The A12 patches the captain over the intercom. "Captain, Peterson and

Hartford are dead" "What the hell happened" It was a Creature Captain"

"Hopkins admit" "Inform all 12s on board to be on the lookout for him"

"Yes captain" The A12s communicate with each other using brain waves all

On board the Boarding ship and the main ship in orbit are informed.

The Commander takes the ship up instantly back through the atmosphere to the

Main ship. She hails for the doctor over the intercom. "Yes Commander is there

Problem. "Yes Doctor the rest of the crew are dead it was Hopkins he has

Transformed Doctor, be on the lookout and come to the control room, as soon as

We dock with the main ship we will lock this ship down and keep him aboard

This ship" "I was afraid of this Commander" "It was in my mind but I did not

Want to think about it Doctor, get up here as soon as you can and be careful"

The doctor grabs a weapon and goes out the door into the hallway. He walks

Toward the control room as softly as he can. He thinks to himself to make as little

Noise as possible. He makes it to the control room easily without any trouble.

He enters the control room. "Glad you could make it doctor buckle yourself in and

Hold on and keep an eye on that door". The commander pilots the ship with ease

Back into the main ship. She lands with no trouble. "Ok Doctor let's get out of

Here lets pray the ships engine are back online" The A12s on board had been

Working on engine this whole time. Doctor let's get off this ship and out of this

Orbit and back to earth in one piece". They open the door from the control room

And slowly step out into the hallway. "I See no one Commander" They walk to the

Main door of the smaller ship. "We made it captain we are going to make it"

At that moment the wolf drops out of the airshaft above, right on top of them

He goes for the doctor grabbing him. He bites into his neck. Blood sprays across

The Commanders face. Commander Patterson hits the exit door switch in the smaller ship

And dives out the door, but the wolf with its long reach nicks her leg with its

Razor sharp nails. The door closes instantly and the wolf is in lock down

In the smaller ship. The captain does not realize she has been infected she was

So worked up and it was just a nick on her leg. The captain runs to the engine

Room. The A12s have did what they could to the engine they are not sure if it

Will work but they did all they could. They inform the captain of their work.

She runs out of the engine room and heads to the main control room buckles in

The pilots chair begins the prep as quickly as her can. She connects her head

Set to begin the trip. She says to herself I Sure hope this works. She hits the

Switch on her monitor. The ship disappears out of orbit. Across the universe the

Ship pops into orbit around earth. The Commander thinks to herself I made it thank

God. She gets out of her chair not checking her instruments. She heads to the

Docking bay where she plans to take a smaller ship to earth's surface. Back in

The control room on the monitor the dates reads the year 1575 but the Commander

Does not know this.

The Commander enters one of the smaller ships goes straight for the control room

She straps in the chair. Without prepping she takes the ship out of the main

Hanger out into orbit. She starts to hail ground base but there is no response

"Dam I'll have to go down in the dark". She looks at the map on her screen it

Shows she is coming down right around Romania

She thinks to herself how Ironic. Halfway down her ship starts to break

Apart but she holds it long enough to make it down. She crashes into the sea

Close to shore. It's a floater ship but it will not stay afloat for long

She makes it out and swims to shore. Exhausted now she lays on the shore

She thinks she should be freezing but she is not she passes out. When she

Wakes up she looks around to see if the ship is still floating but it's done

Gone under. Commander Frost was a survival expert she is not worried about
being

Lost she had been to this part of the country before she knows that the ship

Is sending out a distress beacon. What she does not know is that it's the year

1575. She starts walking toward and over the mountains. She starts to feel strange

She looks up at the sky and sees the Moon coming out. She gets an Eire feeling

About it. She walks on but with only a few steps more she falls to her knees

Holding her stomach in pain. She screams with agony. Her voice starts to change

Into a deeper version. She looks back up at the moon .Her eyes change from blue

To green. In five seconds she is fully transformed. She stands to her feet now

Covered with hair from head to toe. She howls at the moon and runs off into

The Forest...

The wolf in her keeps her alive...And so the werewolf legend has begun....

Time trip Chapter 2

By

Jace Watkins

Transylvania Friday Sept 24. 8:09 Am 1575

Alice frost Lay Undiscovered Passed out in a Wood Line by an OLD Cemetery

There Had Been A Full Moon Last Night, she WAS Nude, SHE had Transformed Back

INTO Human. Her Eyes Open. Its A Blur   .she hears voices in the distance.

She Scrambles Awake. She sees people in the cemetery She Hides behind a Tree

The People Are Leavening It Looks As If They Just Had a Funeral

Alice frost Knows What She Must Do

She needs clothes, And They Just Had a Funeral

She Watches As What Looks To Be A few Wagons Leavening

They Never See Her

Frost Goes for the Grave

She Uses the Shovel Left Behind

She Doesn't Know How Long This Spot Will Be Clear

She Works As Fast As She Can

She Digs Down To the Coffin

"I Sure Hope This Is a Girl" frost Says

She opens the coffin

Its A Young Women About frost's Age

She Has On A fine Handmade Dress

Frost Gets the Dress on Alice Cross Is Beautiful

She Tries To Think Of The last time she wore a dress

Frost follows the road out of the cemetery

She stays along the side of the road staying out of the middle

Frost walks on down the road in this beautiful handmade dress...IT is Black with Red Velvet

Trim

She walks for about an Hour .Then sees just up ahead is a Village.

"I Better Be On My Toes" Alice Says

She walks on down the Road Right into the Village

"That Grave Had To Belong To Someone in This Village "Frost Says To Herself

She Sees an old church at the cater of the village

She could see people and there was no cars .only horses and wagons

"Something Is Telling Me This Is Not the Right Year" Frost Says

Alice Frost Spoke 12 Languages and Romanian Was One of Them

"It's now or never" Frost Says

She Sees an Elderly Gentleman Walking down the Street She Goes OVER To him

"Buna dominate domnule, stii ce telefon este?" Frost Said Good morning Sir Do You Know

What a telephone is.

The Elderly Man Gives A Funny Look and SAYS

"ceea ce este de telefon"? The Old Man Said What Is a Telephone

"Yelp it's The Wrong Year "Alice Says to herself

"Este Sir Nimic admiram doar dimineata ..... Există lucru pe aici"? Alice said Nothing Sir I Was Admiring the Morning...Is There Work Here.

"Taverna are nevoie de o gazdă".The Old Man Replied The Tavern Is In Need Of Some one

"Vă mulțumesc domnule" Alice Says Thank You Sir And Passes Him By

Well that went well Alice Thinks to herself

She walks on down the street she comes to this old wooden building on the right side of the

Village with the word Taverna on it out front

"This must be the place maybe I can find shelter tonight" Alice says
to herself

Alice Opens the Door of the tavern, there was only three people in it

And it looked as if they had been there all night

Alice Closes the Door Trying Not to draw anybody's attrition

No one even sees her. She walks up to the bar keep

"Scuza-ma domnule Im în căutarea de muncă" Frost says Excuse
Me Sir, I'm Looking for Work.

"Suntem în nevoie de un Hostess" The bar keeper Who Is A old man
says They Are in need of A hostess

"Voi lua .... Are vin cu o camera?" Alice said she would take
it....Does it come with a room.

"I se va pune pe fila o cameră tocmai a deschis up.you poate începe
chiar acum de la 6 dimineața până la 6 seara" The bar keep says I
Will put it on your tab a room has just opened up. You can start right

now from 6 in the morning to 5 in the evening.

"Această modalitate de camera dvs"the old man says this way to your room

Alice Frost follows The Old man up a set of stairs they walk down a hallway they come

To the third door

"acest lucru este" This is it the old man says

"Datorită Cobor într-un minut" Alice says she will be down in a moment

She steps into the room and closes the door behind her.

There's a bed and a dresser that's about it...

Frost Sits On The bed

She Just Now Realizes That She no Longer has her Light Weapon

"Maybe I Can Back Track" Alice thinks

"Tonight after Work, I'll get a Light and Go Back"

"I need to find out what year it is."

There's a knock at the door

Alice rises and gets the door

Standing there is a young women about 39

"Sunt aici pentru a afișa datoria ta Young Women Says I'm Here to Show You to Your

Duties".

"Sunt gata .. Tu să-mi spui Alice Says I'M Ready ...YOU Can Call Me Alice.

"ma puteti suna DACIANA" The Young Women Says You Can Call Me DACIANA"

"DACIANA E frumos să te cunosc" Frost Says IT'S nice To Meet

You DACIANA.

"Vă sunt de la aici? DACIANA Says Are You from Here

"Oh, am ajuns chiar" Alice Says Oh I Just ARRIVED.

"bine pe aici" DACIANA SAYS well Right This WAY

DACIANA was A TALL dark HAIRD women About 39

THE TWO WALK down the hall and down the stair case

 They reach the main bar floor There's a candle chandler hanging in the center of the room

"Treaba ta este de a oamenilor de siguranță și asigurați-vă că alții sunt de lucru" DACIANA Says "Your job is to seat people and make sure others are working".

"GREAT I'm going to fit right in" Alice Says

In A Transylvanian Accent " You Speak English, Are You from the New World"? DACIANA Says

"YES but do not tell anyone " Alice says

"Will Tell No One" DACIANA Says

"Aici ne sunt doar du-te la uşă când cineva ajunge" DACIANA says
"Here We Are JUST go to THE door WHEN someone arrives"

AT THAT moment the DOOR opened, IN walked an older
gentleman

"OK, du-te-l scaun" DACIANA Says ok go seat Him.

Alice walks over to the Man WHO is dressed in a hand made black
suit

He is wearing a black hat

"Ce ai nevoie Sir" Alice says "What do you need sir"

"Voi lua o bea bere" THE man SAID" I'll Take A Drink BEER"

"Doar stai oriunde te voi lua o bere" Alice says "Just sit anywhere
I'll Get YOU a beer".

THE man sits down at one of the tables

Alice walks over to the Bar Keep

"Am nevoie de o bere" Alice Says" I Need a Beer"

The bar keep fills her a glass of alcohol and hands it to her

 Takes the class of alcohol from the bar keep and walks it to the table where the man

Is sitting. She sits it in front of him. He Hands Her A coin She Takes It.

She looks at the coin she sees a Date......"1575" Alice Says

"I Need to Find That Weapon" Alice Says to herself

She Walks Back To the Bar KEEP and Hands Him the Coin

HE hands Her Back Two Smaller Coins

"te pe lucreze într-o orǎ .... aici te duci" The Bar Keep Says   " you get off work in an hour....here you go"

"mulțumiri" "Thanks" Alice Says

SHE walks back to the table and hands the man the two smaller coins

"altceva" Anything Else Alice Says

"Sunt bine pentru acum, datoritǎ" The Man Says "I'M fine for now thanks".

"Suna dacǎ ai nevoie de ceva" "Call if you need anything" Alice Says

It will be 6:00 PM in A HOUR Stacey goes back to the bar and sits down

"I got to find a light" Alice says to herself

Alice gets out of her seat and heads for the back room

She comes to the last door down an old hall way

And finally finds what she is looking for it's a lantern it

has a candle in it

"This is what I'll use to back track when it gets dark
"Alice says to herself

She lays the lantern back down and goes back to the
main bar floor

THE man that was drinking has left she goes over to the
table

There is a coin laying on the table Alice picks it up

She puts the coin in her pocket

6:00 pm Transylvania

Alice had got work at the local tavern, she planned on back tracking
to try and find her light weapon WHEN she got off work

Alice exits The Tavern with Lenten Lit In Hand

The sun is coming down it's just over the trees

Alice WALKS down the street and back out of the village and back down the road

The way she came. She walks for about an hour and comes to the cemetery

Its 7:08 PM. the sun has set.It is musky dark

But Alice sees fine and she's not getting that much light from the lantern

It's a Sid effect of the werewolf virus she has in her body

Her senses are heightened she can see in the dark she can hear twigs breaking in the woods at 500 yards away

Alice back tracks for hour's .she just went to the place she woke up from and headed north

She sees another light in the distance. She can hear voices

Its two people

She hears a voice say loudly "Bunǎ ziua acolo" "Hello over there" the voice says

"Alo" "Hello" Alice says

The two party's evenly meet. Its two young women .They are dressed in lesser fine

Clothes than Alice....

"noapte buna" "Goodnight to YOU" one of the girls say

"noapte buna" "GOODNIGHT to you" Lacey says

"SUNT DORINA CE ESTE NUMELE TĂU"? I'M DORINA WHATS YOUR NAME THE GIRL SAYS.

"Alice Frost"

"E frumps aS the Alice Frost "întâlni" the girl says "It's Nice to Meet You Alice Frost" "esti din satul?" "Are you from the village" the girl says

"Da, lucrez în taverna Sunt nou" "YES I WORK AT THE TAVERN I'm New"

Alice looks at the other girl she notices she is carry her uniform

"unde l-ai luat" Frost says "Where Did You Get That"

"l-am găsit doar pe de altă parte munte este rupt" "we found it just on the other mountain it's torn" the girl says

"Ai găsit altceva" "Did you find anything else" Alice says

"doar acest lucru strălucitor nu știm ce este" "Just this shiny thing we don't know what it is" The other girl says

In the hands of the other girl is Alice Frosts light weapon But It WILL not fire unless Alice holding it...It's a Security feature in the weapon

"Vrei SA vinzi că voi da această monedă și o place pe zi, timp de patru zile" "Do you want to sell that I'LL give you this coin and one like it a day for five days Frost Says

"Cenci zine" "FIVE DAYS" the girl says

"Duane lucre in tavern vein de la 18:00 in fiacre zip" "Deal I work in the tavern come by at 6:00 pm each day" Frost says

She Hands the Girl the Coin and Takes the light Weapon from Her

"Eu "M ILEANA I" Ne vedem mâine la 6"...."I'M ILEANA I'll See You Tomorrow at 6" The girl says

"Ne vedem atunci ILEANA" "I'LL see you then ILEANA" Alice says

The two party's pass by...........Alice checks the charge on the weapon

It's almost fully charged

The weapon is on auto safety it can't go off unless Alice grips it and pulls the trigger

She sticks the weapon in her undergarments

She can still see the light from the two girls walking down the road

It's a cool crisp night it is a little cloudy

The clouds start receding .The moon is exposed now

Alice is about 300 yards behind the girls on the road

Alice looks up at the Moon She starts TO feel Funny

"It's Happening I can Feel It.....I'm Transforming....It Must Be the Moon That Triggers It"

"I have to get out of these clothes and remember this spot"

Alice undresses in the dark she blows the candle out. It's all she can do to get out of her clothes And Hide Them She Marks the Spot Mentally

She falls to her knees, Now Nude She Screams in Pain Holding Her Stomach

Her Eyes Turn From Blue to Green

Hair Starts To Grow Rapidly All Over Her Body

Her Screams Now Are a Deep Moan

Her Leg Bones Break and Reform

Muscle Forms .Now standing 6 and a half feet Alice stands Fully Transformed

The Wolf Howls at the Moon...AHOOOL!!

About 300 yards up the road

"Ce a fost asta" ILEANA Says "WHAT was that"

"Nu știu să păstreze în mișcare" "I Don't Know Lets Keep Moving" DORINA Says

The Two walk on down the road

They Hear Nothing

They Walk For About Five Minutes

THE two hear a twig Break In front of them

"Salut Whos Nu" ILEANA says "Hello Who's there"

No Answer

Dorina Holds Her Lantern Up Further So She Can See If She Can
See Anybody

She Can See About Ten Feet In Front Of Her

THE Wolf Springs Fourth, Pouncing On Dorina..She Screams But Is
Killed Almost

Instantly

Ileana Runs Off Screaming

Ileana runs down the Road for Her Life She doesn't Know if that
thing is following her

The Wolf Sits On All Fours Over The Body of Dorina And
Howls...AHWool!!!! The Moon Is In the Distance

DORINA is ripped from chest to throat

The Wolf Stands To Two Feet Gives Another Howl...Ahwoool!!!

And runs off all fours into the
woods...you hear another
Ahwooool!!!! In the distance......

10:35 pm Transylvania

ILEANA has made it back to the village she runs down the street
yelling Help Help

Several people gather around her

"ceea ce este fata problema"? This man said "what's the matter girl"

ILEANA Was out of breath

"Dor...Dorina a fost atacat de o creatura" "Dor....Dorina Has Been
Attacked by a Creature" ILEANA Says

"Acesta a fost de 7 metri cu părul şi de brici ascuţit dinţii şi
ghearele" "It Was 7 Feet Tall

With Hair All over It and Had Razor Sharp Teeth AND claws"
Ileana Says out Of Breath

"Cred că este mort" "I think she is dead" Ileana says

"ORICINE luați armele .. SĂ NE GASITI această creatură"
"EVERYONE GRAB YOUR GUNS ...LET US FIND THIS
CREATURE" One man says

People scatter going in all directions within 4 minutes there are
about 10 armed men in the

Street

"Hai să găsim dorina" "Let's go find dorina" One of the Men Says

The Party Consisted Of Ten Grown Men All Armed With Rifles and
Pistols

The group walked out of the village and down the road and out of
the village

The group walked for about an hour on the road

The group comes along the spot where the attack was

Dorina lay dead lifeless

They examine the body

""Ea a fost rupt de la piept la gât ceea ce în creația lui Dumnezeu ar fi putut face acest lucru........." "She has been torn from her chest to her throat what in God's Creation Could Have done this"   One of the men say

"Numele lui Dumnezeu" "God's Sake" One Man Says

They hear a howl off in the distance

AHWOOOL!!!!   AHWOOOOOOL!!!!

"Ce-a fost un lup ... doar pe de altă parte acelui munte" "WHAT WAS THAT A WOLF...IT'S JUST ON THE OTHER SIDE OF THAT MOUNTAIN". One of the Men Says

"Să se răspândească și să facă o unitate pentru a vedea dacă vom vedea anythin."...."Let's spread out and do a drive to see if we see anything"...another man says

The group spreads out about 50 yards apart from each other and start walking out in the woods

Toward where the howls came. They walk for about 30 minutes
.they can see each other's lights

But that's about it

A GUN shot...........BANG!!!!

A LIGHT drops To the Ground

It was one of the Men on the End. The Other Men Run To the Light

Laying On the Ground. When They Get There They Find Gargling
Blood

HIS throat had Been Ripped out...

"El plecat ... El mort ..... trebuie să aibă indiferent de faptul că urlă
trecut" "He's gone...He's Dead.....It Must Have Been Whatever That
Howled" one man said

"Să adune mort și capul înapoi Town"   "Let's Gather the Dead and
Head Back To The village" The man holding a long rifel Says

At That Moment the WOLF springs into the group of 9 men standing over the dead body

The Wolf Destroys Three Of The Men In under Five Seconds. There Are Gun Shots

BANG!!!   BANG!!! BANG!!! Balm Balm Boom BANG!!!!

THE other 6 men turn a Start to run down the Side of the Mountain

The Wolf Chases After Them, Running On All Fours At Times.....

One Man Drops His Light But The Man Keeps Going.....

The Wolf Leaps At Top Speed and Lands on the Back of One of the Men in the Rear

Of The Group

The Wolf Bites Into His Neck And Then Gives A Howl.......AHWOOOOLL!!!!!!!!!!!

AWOOOOOOOOOOOOOOOOOOOOLLLL!!!!!!!!!!!!!!..

The Other Five Men Make It to the Road They Keep Running All The Way to the Village

"Cred că am de gând să facă el ...... de a nu ne urmărește anymore". I Think We Are Going To Make IT......its Not Chasing Us Anymore the Man In Front Says

"Ce naiba a fost asta" ...What the Hell Was That the man in the rear says

"A fost un fel de uriaș Wolf" "It Was Some Kind Of Giant Wolf" The Man with the Long Rifle Says

The Five Men Finally Slow To a Walk As They Enter the Main Street to the Village

"Eu zic să ne întoarcem First Light și de a recupera mort .... și a vedea dacă există urme" I Say We Go Back First Light And Recover The Dead....And See If There's Any Tracks One Of The Five Men Say

"Du-te informeze toți știți de ce sa întâmplat și să avertizeze oamenii să rămână în afara pericolului fel de mult, deoarece acestea pot până când vom putea ucide aceasta creatura"...Go Inform All You Know Of What Has Happened And Warn People To Stay Out Of The Woods As Much As They Can Until We Can Kill This Creature The Man With The Long Rifle Says

The Five Men Scramble In From The Streets As If A Monster Was Chaseing Them..........

1575 Sat Sept 24 7:32 AM in the Forest Just Outside Of Transylvania

Alice Lay Again Nude Passed Out In the Forest Not Far From the Original Attack

She Awakes

"Brother Not This Again" Alice Says Aloud

She Rises To Her Feet, Feeling Uncomfortable Being Nude

She Sees the Road...She knows where Her Clothes are From Here

Alice Walks Along the Road Staying Back In The woods until she

Comes To the Spot Where Her Clothes Are At

Alice Gets Dressed, Her Light Weapon Is still in her Undergarments

Just as Alice Slips Her Shoes on she hears A Horse Coming down
the Road

It's a young man about Alice's Age He Is Riding a Black Horse

He Comes To a Stop As Comes To Frost

"Salut ...... Ar fi bine să văd de te o fată și cinci oameni au fost uciși
aici doar ca Ultima noapte .. un fel de Creature"............Hello There
......You Better Be Minding Yourself a Girl and Five Men Were
Killed Here Just Last Night ...Some Kind Of Creature" The Young
Man On the Horse Said

"O creatură ce spui ..... A văzut cineva obține un bun privire la
ea"?"A Creature You Say.....Did Anybody Get a Good Look at It"?

"Da șase persoane văzut-Up Close Ei Drescribed ca fiind înalt păros
și cu dinți și gheare ascuțite ras .. Nu este o vânătoare chiar acum în
căutarea pentru el .... Ar fi bine să se întoarce în satul tău Alice de
dreapta ... am fost în Taverna Când au angajat ..... eu sunt Michael
Pătrașcu"........Yes People Saw It up Close They Described it as
being tall hairy and with razor sharp teeth and claws. There Is A
Hunting Party Out Right Now Looking For It....You Better Be
Heading Back To the Village Your Alice Right...I Was In The
Tavern When They Hired you.....I'M Michael

.

"Ei bine, mulțumim Michael voi fi la rubrica înapoi la sat i-au de lucru"...Well Thanks Michael I'll be heading back to the village I have work"

"OK Alice Michael Says

The Horse Gallops On Down the Road

Alice Try's to remember what happened

She can't

She starts to walk down the road back to the village

She walks for about an hour and makes in To the Village at 9:23 Am

She walks into the tavern at 9.27 she was supposed to be at work at 6:00 am

She goes inside but sees no one everyone is at a meeting at the village center

She walks the stair case to her room she opens the door and enters

Alice lays on the bed and falls asleep

An hour passes.............there's a knock at the door........KNOCK!!!

Alice Awakes suddenly

She fixes her hair the best she can there is no mirror in the room

She opens the door

It's DACIANA

"Bună dimineața Alice" "Good morning Alice" DACIANA Says

"Nici o lucrare astăzi, din cauza unui partid de vânătoare ....
Șase persoane au fost ucise aseară în pădure cu un fel de
creatură"........No work today because of a hunting party................
Six people were killed last night in the forest by some kind of
creature" DACIANA Says

"Cineva cunoscut"...."Anyone You Know" Alice Says

"Dorina" DACIANA says

Alice's Face Goes To A Blank Stare ....Dorina. She Thinks To Herself And

Remembers the Girl from Last Night

Alice Comes Out Of Her Door and Daciana Follows Her down The Hall

"So there's No Work Today" Alice says

In a Transylvanian Accent Dacanay Replies "No Everyone Is In the Hunting Party"

I'm going out for A Bit I'll Be Back Later "Alice says

Transylvanian Accent ..."They are warning People to Stay Away from Forest" Danica Says

"I'M Just Going to Look around I Won't Be Gone Long "Alice Says

Alice Frost Walks Out Of the Tavern and Onto the Street of Transylvania

She Walks by the Old Church Alice Had Been To This Church In 2024

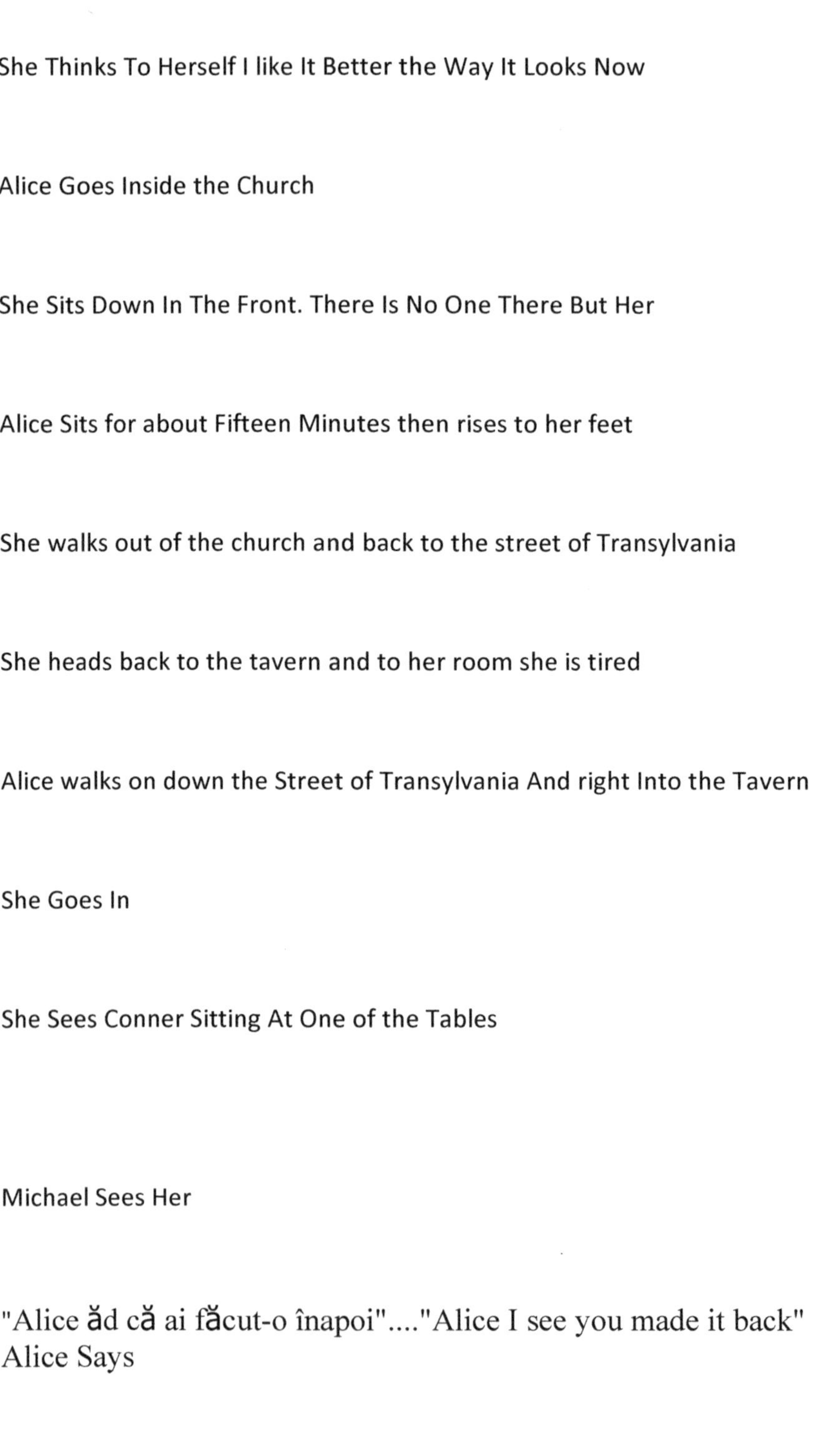

She Thinks To Herself I like It Better the Way It Looks Now

Alice Goes Inside the Church

She Sits Down In The Front. There Is No One There But Her

Alice Sits for about Fifteen Minutes then rises to her feet

She walks out of the church and back to the street of Transylvania

She heads back to the tavern and to her room she is tired

Alice walks on down the Street of Transylvania And right Into the Tavern

She Goes In

She Sees Conner Sitting At One of the Tables

Michael Sees Her

"Alice ăd că ai făcut-o înapoi"...."Alice I see you made it back"
Alice Says

"Da, sunt bine ..... Am crezut că acest loc a fost închisă astăzi"..."Yes I'm Fine.....I Thought This Place Was Closed Today" Alice Says

"Este ... eu doar oprit pentru o băutură"..It Is...I Just Stopped By For A Drink" Michael Says.

Alice Sits Down At The Table.....

"Spune-mi despre tine Alice"...."Tell Me about Yourself Alice" Michael Says

"Nu e nimic de spus intr-adevar I'm 27 am ajuns doar vineri"......"There's Nothing To Really Say I'm 27 I just Arrived Friday" Alice Says

"Și unde ești de la Alice"...."And where are you from Alice?" Micheal Says

Alice thinks to herself she better tell him she is from the new world DACIANA Already Knows

"Sunt din America de"......"I'M from the new world" Frost Says

"You Alice Are From the new world?"   Michael says in a thick

Transylvanian accent

"Just Arrived Friday" Alice says

"From what part are you from Alice" Michael says in a thick accent

Alice thinks to herself what existed in America in 1575

"I'm From Virginal" Alice says

"Did you like the new world?" Alice says

"Yes I Love It" Alice says

"Why did you leave?" Michael says in a thick accent

"To see the world" Alice says

"And you choose Romania out of all the places to go" Michael says

"I have always wanted to see this country" Alice says

"What you Think So far?" Michael says

"I Love it................ beautiful country" Alice says

"Glad to hear you like   Alice" Michael says

"You speak English pretty good Michael where did you pick that up?" Alice says

"Little here little there I pick up." Michael says
"I Do Good Yes"

"You would fit right in Micheal." Alice says

"Thanks Alice" Michael says

"You want more drink   Michael" Alice says

"One more then I have business to attend to" Michael says

Alice Grasp his glass and takes it behind the bar and fills his glass

It's just her and Michael in the tavern.

Alice walks back over to the table a sits Michael's glass down

"Most Thanks Alice" Michael says

Michael Drinks up his drink in a hurry

"I Will See You Alice from Virginal" Michael says

"I will see you Michael" Alice says

"You stay clear of the forest for the time being ok Alice" Michael says

"Will do Michael" Alice says

Michael lays two coins on the table for the drinks

"And this is for you" Michael says handing Alice A Larger Coin

"Thanks Michael" Alice says

I'm Michael Viteazu

Michael stands up and walks out of the tavern

Alice puts the large coin in her pocket and takes the two smaller coins and lays them

On the bar...........Alice is alone now.....she thinks to herself Viteazu ..That Guy Is a Prince.....Michael the Brave" Alice says in amazement

 Alice heads up the staircase to her room

 She opens the door and goes inside close the door behind her

 Alice Lays down on the bed she is asleep within sixty seconds

 Hours pass

 There's a knock at the door KNOCK!!! KNOCK!!! KNOCK!!!

 Alice Wakes suddenly

 "Be Right There "Alice says

She opens the door it's DACIANA

"Hello Alice" DACIANA says in a thick Transylvanian accent

"Hello DACIANA" Alice says....."Come in"

DACIANA walks into the room

"So Alice How Do You like Transylvania?" DACIANA says in a thick accent

Alice thinks to herself well so far it's not been great for me

"I Love it Danica" Alice says

"Have you looked in the closet yet" Danica says in a thick accent

Alice had not looked in the closet.

"NO what's in there?" Alice says

Daciana goes to the closet door and opens it

It's full of clothes a whole wardrobe is in there

"These belonged to Violeta she died recently she had no family she was about your age you can have these clothes" Daciana says

"Thanks Daciana" Alice says...."I'll take them"

Alice searches through the clothes and finds a more suitable attire

Something less fancy. She changes right in front of Daciana

Now Alice had on a cream color dress just plain no trim

It was five forty seven PM the sun was coming down

"You have a goodnight Alice of the new world "Daciana says in a thick accent

"You too Dacinan have a goodnight" Frost says

Daciana leaves the room...

Alice goes to the window and looks out

"It will be dark soon" Alice says to herself

"I have to head for the forest. Can't afford transforming right here in my room" Alice says

Alice in a cream color dress now exits her room and heads downstairs

She comes to the main bar floor...doesn't even bother getting a lantern

Walks out the door and into the street of Transylvania

Alice walks down the street. She thinks to herself she has not eaten since she got here

But she was not hungry ...Another side effect from the werewolf virus

She does not eat...not like a human anyway...Alice by day Wolf by night

She's blood thirsty when she is the Wolf...That's when she feeds....Blood.

Alice is not carrying her light weapon she hid it in the closet. She couldn't risk

Loosening it when she transformed. Alice walks by an older gentlemen with an old hat

And old clothes...

"Ce mai faci domnule"...how are you sir "Alice says

"Sunt bine cue faci"...."I'm fine how are you" the old man says in the old hat and brown clothes

The two pass each other by one going one direction one going the other

Alice walks on down the street. There are old wooden buildings on both side of the street

She thinks to herself if I can get further back in the forest maybe nobody will get killed

Its 6:32 pm the sun is down close to the mountains. Alice walks on out of the village

And down the road she comes to the cemetery at 7:02 pm its dark now but the moon is not out

Alice comes to the spot where she originally woke up...

She continues on down the road past the cemetery she walks for about two hours

Its 9:02pm now but still no moon...Alice continues down the road she makes it farther than she has ever been

She leaves the road undresses hides her clothes...she marks the spot mentally

Alice now Nude walks up the side of a mountain. Alice is not tired at all

Another side effect from the werewolf virus

It's a cool crisp night again but Alice is not cold she feels so Alive

Her blood is pumping heart racing her adrenaline is pumping

All side effects from the virus

Alice comes to the top of the mountain and sits down on a log

"Maybe this will be good enough "Alice says

She waits...an hour passes

It's now 10:15pm the clouds start to reread Alice can see light behind the clouds

"Well this is it "Alice says

Another 20 seconds go by The Moon starts to show itself

Another 15 seconds and the moon is fully exposed

"I Can feel it I hate this" Alice says

Alice...Nude...rises from her seat stumbles around

She falls to her knees screaming in pain holding her stomach

"OH GOD OHHHHHHH" Alice screams

On all fours Alice starts to transform. Her hair starts to grow rapidly

Her face and nose start to grow her eyes turn from blue to green

Her leg bones break and reform

"OH GOD OHHHHHH" in a deeper voce now

Muscle form...the transformation is complete Alice Is Now the Wolf

Sitting on all fours the wolf gives a howl at the moon

Ahwoooollll!!!!!!!   Alwoooooooooolll!!!!!

The wolf takes off down the mountain side at high speed it makes
the road with in minutes

It is now 10:20pm down by the cemetery on the road came a wagon
heading for Wallachia

It was a family of four the wagon consisted of an older man about 53
named Alexandra

His two sons Anton 16 and Aurel 14 and their mother Stela 49
Alexandra is driving the wagon

He wipes the horses to move along they pass the cemetery they are heading right for THE WOLF

The wagon makes it to the clearing they get about half way through the clearing

AHWOOOOOLLL!!!!!!!

"ceea ce a fost că"?...."what was that" Stela says to Alexandra

"Eu nu știu Stela dar ne păstrăm mai bine în mișcare"....."I do not know Stela but we better keep moving" Alexandra says

The wagon moves on down the road and passes the clearing...then another howl

Ahwoooollll!!!!!!! Closer this time just up ahead

Alexandra stops the wagon ...they listen they hear nothing

"Stela dă-mi pușca de la partea din spate a vagonului"...."Stela give me the rifle from the back of the Wagon" Alexandra says

Stela goes in the back of the wagon digs around and finds the rifle ...it's an ancient weapon

Looks to be two hundred years old its black powder and its loaded

Stela hands the ancient weapon to Alexandra

The two boys are talking to each other they have no intrest in what's going on

AHWOOOOOOOOLL!!!!!

Another howl just yards in front of them but their lantern is very weak they can only see about

Five feet ahead .The two boys are at attition now....Alexandra stands in the wagon with his rifle

Pointed straight ahead Stela sits in the seat next to him.....

Twigs break they see movement in the light of their lantern

The Wolf springs onto the wagon it lands on top of Stela it bites in her throat

Blood sprays everywhere. Alexandra turns his ancient weapon and fires...

He hits the Wolf square in the chest.

"rula băieți rula".....'"Run boys run" Alexandra says scrambling for his knife on his belt

The two boys jump out of the wagon and start running down the road back toward the village

Alexandra stands with a 14 inch knife in his hand he is still in the wagon

The Wolf is devouring Stela who is dead

Alexandra stabs at The Wolf. His bald finds its mark

He stabs the Wolf 7 times before it leaves Stela's dead body The Wolf turns

For Alexandra

The Wolf Swipes At him with its razor sharp claws striking Alexandra across the face

Alexandra is bleeding profusely from his face he can barely stand

He manages to stab the wolf one more time but it has no effect on the Wolf

The Wolf goes for Alexandra's throat...it bits into him...blood spraying everywhere

Alexandra is dead within seconds...The Wolf lapping at the blood flowing from the neck wound

The Wolf gives a howl.

Ahwooooooooolll!!!!!

The two boys make it to the cemetery they keep running as fast as they can

They run down the road for about twenty minutes and slow to a fast walk

They walk on down the road they will reach the village in five minutes

AHWOOOOOOOOLLL!!!!!! Off in the distance

THE TWO boys make it to the village its 11:47pm the moon is high in the sky

Aurel screams......."ajută să ne ajute SUA!! "

"Help us HELP US!!!!"

The man that carry's the long rifle comes running out weapon in hand

""CE ESTE BOY"..."WHAT IS IT BOY" The man says

"Mama și tatăl nostru a fost atacat a fost creatura"...."our mother and father have been attacked it was the creature" Aurel says

"Băieții merg la casa vărului tău voi doi sta aici la noapte mă duc sa o caut pe mama și pe tatăl tău"......"Boys go to your cousin's house you two stay here tonight I will go look for your mother and father" The man with the long rifle says

The two boys run on down the street and goes into one of the smaller buildings there was candle light on inside

 Beniamin the man with the long rifle goes to the center of the village .there's a bell there

Beniamin starts to ring the bell.......DONG!!!   DONG!!!! DONG!!!

Doors open and people start coming out

"toată lumea vin aici"....."Everybody come here"...Beniamin says ....holding his long rifle in hand

"There's fost un atac Alexandra și Stela Robling Thier doi băieți să se întoarcă în sat .... Să ne aduna o petrecere de vânătoare mai mare și du-te uita pentru această creatură lup"......."There's been another attack Alexandra and stela Robling their two boys made it back to the village....Let us gather a larger hunting party and go look for this wolf creature" Beniamin says

It is now 12:15pm about twenty men Conner *was one of the men.*

All The men was armed with swords and rifles and pistols

They get on horses and head out of the village

By 12:40 they reach the attack site they find the bodies of Alexandra and Stela

Alexandra lay half way off the wagon there's a pool of blood on the ground where

He bled out. Stela seated in the wagon...Dead...her throat torn out

"Căci tot ce este sfânt .. Trebuie să ucidem chestia asta și rapid"..."For all that is holy. We must kill this thing and fast" Michael says aloud

Every other man is carrying a lantern. They are all on horses

"Permite împărțit în doi câte doi, putem acoperi mai multe puști și pistoale de la sol a nu afecta pe creatura încerca și a tăiat capul off cu sabia"......Lets split up into twos we can cover more ground rifles and pistols has no effect on the wolf

AHWOOOOOOOLL!!!!! In the far distance

"Asta e ... Se pare ca sa pe cealaltă parte a muntelui ..... Să Mutare în acest fel ... Amintiți-vă ce va trebui să utilizeze săbiile".........."That's It ...It sounds as if it's on The other side of the Mountain.....Lets Move that way...Remember you will have to use your swords" Michael says

The group of men all go in twos in different directions but in the same direction as the howl

There are ten Lights and Twenty men

They Travel up and over the mountain

They move swiftly up the mountain side on their horses

Michael is on the east of the mountain with his rider and light

A Howl

Ahwoooooll!!!!

Michael says and points to Paul's left

Paul rides over to the left Michael follows up the rear. Paul is holding the lantern. A GUN SHOT..... BANG!!

Michael is about 20 feet behind Paul...he trots over to Paul ...."ceea ce a fost Pavel"...."wat was the paul" Michael says

"a fost doar un oposum"....."It was just a possum" Paul says

From the light of their lantern they see a possum about ten feet in front of them.

Another gun shot off in the distance...all most on the other mountain

Michael and Paul Gallop up and over the mountain toward the gun shot

They see a light in the distance...with swords drawn they gallop up
the light

A Man lay dying garlgulying blood

Paul; and Michael go to the dying man

"Aces om nu este în grupul nostru ..... este George ... Nici măcar nu
e înarmat"....."This man is not in our group.....is George...". Michael
says

A Howl off in the distance

AWHOOOOOOLL!!!!!!

"Unde este Wolf?" ..."Where is that Wolf?" Paul says

"Asti Este ceca cue no numen canasta creature un vârcolac"...."That
is what we will call this creature a werewolf" Michael
says....................Another howl

AHWOOOOOOLL!!!!!! Off in the distance about 400 yards to the north

"Hai să mergem, vom veni înapoi și să obțină prima lumină George
.... Ține sabia afară ."..."Come on let's go we will come back and
get George first light........Keep your sword out.."

Another howl as the two horses trot off up the other mountain.

Awhoooooolll!!!!!!!!.........

AWHOOOOOOOLL!!!!!!!

The two gallop on up the mountain...swords in hand

The Moon Shines Brightly over
Head.....................AWHOOOOOLLL!!!!!!!!!!!!!!!

Wolf Spike Chapter 3

Written By

Jace Watkins

Michael and Paul Have Rode Deep Into the forest .Further Than Anybody Else

Has gone. The Rest of the Hunting Party Are on The Second Mountain Behind them

They Reach The Top Of The Mountain They Are Traveling On.

The Two Come To A Stop. They Both Have Swords Drawn

Paul Holds His Lantern Up High Over Head. Light shines from the lantern about ten

Feet in front of them. They See and Hear Nothing

"A fost ore de când am auzit că Mihai cred că a plecat din zonă"..."it's Been Hours Since We Heard It Michael I Believe It Has Left The Area" Paul says To Michael

"Să mai așteptăm aici pentru câteva momente Paul"...."Let's Wait Here For A Few Moments Paul". Michael says In a Soft Voice.

The two sit on top of their horses on top of the largest mountain in the area

The Moon Shines Brightly Overhead. They Hear Nothing

Michael Pats His Horse on the Neck and Says

"ușor Fata".."Easy Girl"

Both horses was uneasy, making a snorting noise

The Horses Move Around staying in almost the same place they were standing

Paul still holding the lantern high overhead. The Two Can See about 10 Feet In Front of them

They See Nothing. Michael Gets Off His Horse Sword In Hand. Its A Well Designed Weapon .The blade was pure silver

The sword was just at 100 years old it had belonged to Michael's Great Grandfather

Michael walks out in the Distance about Five feet. He can see a little further now with

The Moon Shining Over Head.

The Horses Get Even More Uneasy Snorting and Twisting About .Paul Calms Them Down

"simplu".."Easy" Paul says in a soft voice to the horses

"Haide Michael, Să țină pasul cu restul grupului"..."Come On Michael ,Lets Catch Up With The Rest Of The Group" Paul Says To Michael.

Michael Does Not Say Anything he stands in the same place sword in hand

1 Second

2second

"bine".".Ok" Michael Says A Little Louder

He turns around to begin walking back to his horse

He takes one step and he hears a loud noise coming at him from behind

He turns back around but the second He Turned toward the Noise he is knocked down

Knocked unconscious The Wolf had come at him at top speed... Michael Horse Runs Down the Side of the Mountain at a Gallop

The Wolf had only stabbed Conner in the Chest It Was a Tiny Wound, But Just Enough

The Wolf Rare's To Two Legs and howls

A Gun Shot   BANG!!!!!!!!

A bullet strikes the wolf drawing its attition it spots Paul at about 15 yards away on his horse

The Wolf Leaps, Running on all fours Paul whips his horse and wheels his horse down the side of the mountain

The Wolf Can Hit Forty Miles an Hour in under 5 seconds. It Easley Catches Paul

The wolf leaps into the Air at Top Speed Catching the Hind Quarter of the Horse

The Horse Falls

Paul Hits the Ground Running, but the Wolf Is Traveling Through the Air and Leaps

Onto Him. Knocking him down

The Wolf Bites Into Paul's Neck With Its Massive Jaws Blood Sprays The Wolf Bits A Hunk OF flesh...Half Of Paul's Neck is Gone..........Paul Is Dead.......

The Wolf RISES on its hind legs and howls Teeth showing AHOOOOOLLL!!!!!!!!

The Wolf Drops Back down To Four Legs ....Laps the blood up where Paul had died Gives another Howl   Ahoooooooolll!!!!

The Wolf Takes Off At High Speed down THE Side of the Mountain....Paul Lay Dead

Michael lay unconscious The Wolf Had Left the Area

Michael Lay......Invested......Tomorrow Night He Will Turn Into A Werewolf

You can hear the wolf howling about 500 yards away

8:08AM Sep Sunday 25 1575 deep in the forest of Transylvania

Michael lay sleeping, he feels something licking his face...it's a dog...Michael opens his eyes

..."

"Ok băiat te duci departe"............"Ok boy you go away" Michael Says Sitting up

Michael pushes the dog away and slowly rises to his feet. He picks his sword up laying on the ground. The Moment His Hand Touches The Silver Hand Guards It Starts To Simmer. Michael Drops the Sword

"Rahat".."Shit" Michael Says Out Loud

"Ce dracu '...."What the hell" Michael says

Michael bends over and squats down by the sword, he takes his figure and touches the

Non silver handle, nothing happens. He touches the tip of his finger to the silver blade, His figure

Tip sizzles.

"rahat"...."Shit" Michael says

Michael reaches and grabs the sword by its non-silver handle careful to not touch the silver hand guard's .He Puts the Weapon in Its Scabbed

"Spun nimeni"...Tell No One" Michael says softly

Michael takes off walking down the Mountain Side the Dog Follows Him

He walks about 30 yards and comes across Paul's lifeless mutilated dead body

"Nu Nu Nu sǎraci Paul"

".".no No no poor Paul" Michael says Aloud

Michael Stands Remembering the nose that hit him from behind

Michael feels of his chest, He finds the wound

"Cred ca sunt norocos un Paul"....".I guess I'm lucky a Paul" Michael Says to Paul's Dead Body

Michael walks on down the Side of the Mountain and Back up across another mountain

And down that mountain he walked for about thirty mins and finally made it to the road

He was about an hour away from the village, Michael walks on down the road. He comes to a curve in the road, He walks on around the curve in the road, He Walks right up on in her shoes on

"Alice Ce faci tu aici".. "Alice what are you doing here?" Michael Says In a Thick Accent

Alice Frost Had Just Made It to the Spot Where Her Clothes Was Hidden She Was Startled

She Continues Putting On Her Shoes

"Oh Hey Michael" Frost Says

SHE Finishes Putting On Her Shoes, She Walks Over To Michael

"I was putting Flowers on A Grave, I Had Rocks in My Shoes" Alice Says

"Alice You Really Should Not Be Here, There Was Attacks Last

Night Here My Friend

Paul Lay Dead Not Two Hundred Yards from Here"

"The Creature" Alice says

"I See" Alice Says

"Let's Be Getting to the Village Alice Somethings Happened"
Michael says in a thick accent

"Yeah I'm Late for Work" Alice says

The Two Walk Down the Road for About an Hour And Make the
Village

They walk down the street of Transylvania they make it to the Tavern at
9:54Am

"I Need a Drink" Michael Says In a Thick Accent

The Two walk Into the Bar Alice Goes over to the Bar Keep

"MI pare ray că am întârziat" .."Sorry I'M Late" Alice Says

"Nu e nici o munca de azi Alice"...There's NO WORK TODAY
Alice the old man behind the bar says

"Voi lua doua beri Pune-o în contul meu"....."I'll Take Two Beers
Put It on My Tab Alice says to the old bar keep

The old man fills two mugs full of alcohol and hands it to Alice

Alice takes the glasses and walks over to the table where Michael is
sitting staring off into nothing

"Michael You Ok" Alice says

Michael comes out of his trance   and looks at Alice

"Alice you should have seen what this thing did to Paul" Michael
says in a thick accent

"Michael was you injured in the attack?" Alice ask Michael

"Just a scratch on my chest I was knocked out" Michael says

"Michael you have to come with me tonight" Alice says

"Where are we going Alice?" Michael ask

I'LL explain later here's a beer on me, we need two horses" Michael says

"We can get two from my families stable" Michael says taking the beer from Alice

He drinks his beverage and Alice drinks a little too

"Michael have you noticed any changes you have been experiencing since last night?" Alice Ask Michael

"No"   Michael says sharply

But Michael was lying he had experienced changes, he could no longer touch silver without it burning his hand and Michael could see and hear everything now all side effects from the werewolf virus

The two sit at the table and drink their beer

"Michael somethings going to happen to you tonight" Alice says

"Going to get killed if don't stay out of forest" Michael says in a thick accent

"No Michael you have been infected by the creature that's killing all
these people, you will turn into one of these creatures tonight when
the moon comes out" Alice says calmly

Michael's face goes back to a blank stare, he starts to remember
trying to touch the silver blade

Michael we have to ride deep into the forest tonight we have to try
and get as far away from people as we can"   Alice says

"Alice it will not be safe for you these are Vicious Creatures"

"Michael I'm The Creature" Alice Says softly

"WHAT" Michael Says

"Keep it Down Michael, We are both in this now" Alice Says

"Explain Alice". Michael Says Demandingly

"Michael I'm From the year 2058 I Was part of a mission that goes
to other stars ,on my mission the group that I was with came in
contact with a breed of animal .these "werewolf's" as they are
historically named was all over the planet we went to. I was the only

one that made it back to earth but I traveled in the past I came down to earth in a smaller ship it crashed into the sea I walked over the mountains for an hour and then I remember seeing the moon, hats what triggers the transformation the next thing I remember I woke up in a wood line next to an old cemetery nude .I came here and got work and have been returning to the forest every night. I have been trying to avoid people during my transformation but all these dam hunting party's now there's going to be two wolfs in the forest at night. We have to ride out of this village by night fall" Alice says

"You're from the year 2058, in the future I don't believe you, prove this to me "Michael says in a thick accent in amazement

"Ok Wait Here" Alice says

Alice gets out of her seat and walks upstairs to her room she goes into her room and goes to the closet .she reaches in the top of the closet and grabs her Light weapon she had wrapped up in a shirt.

She takes the weapon and stuffs it in her undergarment and walks out of her door. She walks back down the stairs and on the bar floor. She walks back over to Michael who is finishing up his drink

"Let's go for a walk Michael" Alice says to him

Michael rises up out of his seat he lays 3 coins down on the table

The two walk out of the tavern onto the streets of Transylvania

They walk past the butcher shop, an old man is chopping up a deer on the table as they pass the shop

They cut into one of the alleys past the butcher shop and go in the back of the building

They are now behind the main street behind the buildings no one can see them from here

"Ok Alice from the future what are we doing back here." Michael says in a thick accent

Alice reaches into her undergarments and pulls the silver Metallic Light weapon out

"You see that little bush over there Michael?" Alice says pointing to a derided up little

Shrub bush about 50 feet away

"Yes" Michael says in a thick accent

Alice draws down on the shrub bush and pulls the trigger of the Light pistol A Brilliant Blueish white light ball emerges from the weapon traveling at great speed traveling the 50 feet

Within a second striking the bush setting it to a blaze

Michael stands mouth open in amazement .he reaches for the light weapon taking it from Alice's hands

Michael points the weapon off in the distance and pulls the trigger nothing happens

"It's a security feature in the weapon Michael it will only fire in my hands" Alice says

Michael hands the weapon back to Alice

"2058 You Say" Michael says

"I bet you are home sick "Michael says in a thick accent

"I miss my car, and New York" Alice says

The Two Walk Back To the Main Street

"Alice we are doomed" Michael says in a thick accent as they walk down the street

"we're Not doomed Michael we just have to ride further back in the forest we tie the horse mark the spot mentally take our clothes off walk 100 yards and wait for the moon " Alice says

Some ones coming" Alice says

Walking up on the two was a young man about 34 carrying a rifle it was *Luca*

"Luca ceca cue adduce Zia de as"..."Luca what brings you out today" Michael says

""Am de grand cu un group pentru an aduna pe cei morți în timp ce oamenii săi de avertizare încă lumină acolo, departe de pădure nu partide de vanatoare in seara asta"....."I'm going with a group to gather the dead while its still light there warning people away from the forest no hunting party's tonight" Luca Says To Michael

He passes the two And Alice and Michael keep walking down the street

They walk all the way down past the old church and on past it to the end of the other side of the village

"This Stable Belongs to my family Alice" Michael says in a thick accent

Alice and Michael Walk Through the Stable Barn Door and Go Inside

Its A Large building with exposed rafters from the inside there was ten stalls a few of them had horses in them

"I'm Going to get some sleep Michael I suggest you do the same I'll meet you back here

At Five pm and we will ride out"

"Ok Alice you get some rest" Michael says in a thick accent

5:00pm Sep 25 Sunday 1575 Streets of Transylvania

Alice comes out of the tavern and into the streets of Transylvania she walks

Down past the church and right down the road to the stables she goes inside the stable

Michael is saddling the horses

"Get any sleep Alice" Michael says in a thick accent

"Yeah but it was a strange sleep I kept dreaming I was running in the forest" Alice says

"Here I got us two lanterns "Michael says in a thick accent

"We won't need them Michael we can see in the dark" Alice says

"Michael I have to warn you it's going to hurt when you turn" Alice says

The two mount their horses Alice Now Wearing Pants and a Red and White Shirt

Michael is wearing a black shirt with boots and black pants .The two ride out of the stable and down the street

They leave Transylvania at 5:45pm

11:15 pm deep in the forest

The moon has been out for hour's .On their way back from a short vest to family wealthy man and his

Party make their way over the mountains the man was very sick he had a virus and a common cold

The party consisted of 12 people they was all lightly armed. They was about an hour away from the

 Man's castle .The man sneezes. "Vreau să ajung în camera mea și în pat cât mai curând posibil" "I want to get in my quarters and into bed as soon as possible" The man Says Aloud .

The party rode for about 15 more mins .the two men in lead have lanterns they signal to stop. "ceva se mișcă în fața noastră" "something's moving in front of us" The Man on the Left Said.

The wealthy man was in the middle of the party he was throwing up .A blur of fur comes flying through the air and knocks the man off his horse .the wolfs claws sink into the shoulders of the wealthy man .he passes out from being so sick. The men in the party pull their pistols and starts firing BANG!!! BAM!!!! BOOM!!!

another blur of fur hits the party from in front .the wolf leaves the wealthy man and joins the other wolf in killing all men within 10 seconds the wolfs give a double howl HOOOOOLLL!!!! and run of up the mountain side leaving the wealthy man still alive he lay passed out he had been invested but the wealthy man already had a virus and a common cold the two combined with the werewolf virus had mutated into a new strain there would be no transformation but there was still side effects the wealthy man would now have super human strength .he would not change into a werewolf but the blood lust would still be there he would grow fangs and he is now allergic to the sunlight he also has stopped ageing .he awakes twenty mins later. He feels fine now he is not sick anymore and he could see in the dark now too

He walks up the mountain side and finds one of the horses still alive and ride able he gets on it and makes his way to his castle he will be heartbroken when he realizes he will never see the sun again

6:00 AM Mon 1575 in the forest of Transylvania

Alice and Michael have made it to the spot where their clothes and the horses was tied

They get dressed. "Maybe no one was killed last night Michael we are deep in the forest"

"Remember flashes only glimpse but I think we attacked someone" Michael says

"Les Get Back to the village and find out if there was any attacks." Alice says

They mount their horses and within an hour and a half they make it back to the village

Its 7:30 when they arrive at the village.They head for the stables and put their horses up

Then make their way to the tavern to see if they hear of any news. They walk in the tavern at 7:47 AM the place is packed. "Alice you don't have to do this you don't have to work

My family is rich you can stay at my family home it's just me now you have been through

enough you shouldn't have to put up with this mess let's get a drink and listen to the talk of the day then get your things and we will go to my home" "I'll Take you up on that Michael right now I just want to sleep"

"Go get a table Alice I'll get us some drinks" Michael says

Alice walks to the back of the bar floor and sits down at one of the tables she lays her head down on the table Michael sits Alice's beverage down in front of her.

"I informed the bar keep you would no longer be working here." Michael says with an accent

"Did you hear of any attacks?" Alice ask

"Yes there was a Drake and His party was attacked last night Drake survived he was injured so that's going to be another wolf in the forest"

"Drake?" Alice Ask." I have a funny feeling this Drake is not going to turn into a werewolf

Do you know where he lives? Alice Ask

"Yes he has a castle to the north." Michael says

"We must go see this Drake soon and find out for ourselves if he has the werewolf virus and it's changed him somehow differently .finish your drink Michael I must sleep"

"I'm ready now Alice lets go get your things and be on our way"

They walk up the stairs and go for a storage closet at the top of the stairs

Michael grabs

A large bag to put Alice's clothes in they enter her room Alice takes the bag from Michael

And goes to the closet .she grabs the light pistol and sticks it in her undergarment she takes all of her clothes and puts them in the bag

They walk out of the tavern and walk to the end of the other side of the village where Michael's ancestral home was located. They go inside the door Alice's has never seen anything like it was decorated with weapons of the day there was all kinds of swords suits of armor arrows bows crossbows spears shields what she would call a black jack there was enough weapons here to outfit a small army

"How do you like my home" Michael asks? In an accent

"Unlike anything I've ever saw with my own eyes" Alice says

With this Drake we may be able to become vampires if something about this man has

Changed the werewolf virus then we need to get a hold of that virus we have a better chance if we are vampires. Alice says

"   What's a vampire" Michael says

"it is a form of the same kind of virus your carrying right now but something about This Dark has changed the virus we will no longer turn into werewolf's we will still have our strength and all our ability's and unfourntly we will have to consume blood to stay alive we won't be able to go out in the sunlight but we will live forever and we should be able to control ourselves that's my main reason for this plan we can even leave Transylvania and have a better life if this plan works" Alice says

"Ok so how do we get this virus Alice?" Michael ask

"we either have to get this Drake to bite us or we have to drink some of his blood either way we are getting that new strain of virus because we have a far better shot do you know the location of this castle and do you think it will be guarded well? “Alice says

"Yes it is about a day away by horse back from here he had his best men with him when he was attacked they are all dead it will just be servents." Michael says

"If we reach him before he realizes what he is we might have a chance if it even works we may still turn into werewolf's when the moon is fullest there's no way of really knowing “Alice says

The master clock dongs its 10:00AM with this new plan constructed they intend on getting as much rest as possible and setting off for the castle. Alice intends on using the light pistol if necessary only to wound but she thinks with brute force the two of them can overcome this Drake with ease steal a better slice of immortality and have a better grip on the situation but this is the closest thing to a cure to the werewolf versus

"Show me to a bed Michael I have to sleep" Alice says

"Follow me I'll take you to your room I think you'll find the accommodations here better than your old room" Michael says with his accent

"As long as the beds soft "Alice says

They come to the last door down the hall

"This was one of my sister's room I think you'll find it comfortable Michael says

"Sleep well Alice from the Future"

Alice closes her door

Time Trip

By

Jase Watkins

5:00 pm Mon Sep 1575 Transylvania

Alice is still asleep .she thinks she's in her apartment in New York dreaming .she awakes suddenly

Now realizing that it was all happening she gets dressed as quickly as her can. She leaves her room

She starts walking down the hall of many doors and comes to the main room which is the size o

F a medium house there's a 50 foot ceiling with an upper deck leading to other rooms. Alice is

Standing in history

She walks up to a light suit of armor display she's only seen something like this in a museum or

On TV. She touches it .it was a light outfit the kind made for fast combat it consisted of double

 Stitched steal shirt and pants with a green cape with a golden lion on the back of the cape there

 Was a sword attacked in its scabbed around the waist of the lower armor .Alice pulls the sword

Out of its scabbed the handle of the sword is a leather grip

Alice hasn't held a sword since she was at military school she was a better than average student

In that subject but Alice thinks to herself she has a better weapon than this but this display

 Gives her an idea. She calls for Michael. He comes in from another room

"Alice did you get any rest? "Michael ask

"Michael can I wear this battle armor?

"

"Alice are you planning on fighting a war?

'

"Michael we know this   Drake Has Been Infected by Us .He is going to be cunning he will more than likely refuse

To help us if he knew the truth and I don't know how powerful he will be in reality so our best option is to try and trick him" Alice says staring at the suit of arms on display

"What have you in your mind Alice? "Michael ask

"Do You Have Battle Armor for Horses Here Too? "Alice Ask

"Yes I have many different ones" Michael says

"We pose as royal knights investigating these killings if he believes us he might submit some of his blood if he thinks we are after the creatures "Alice says

"Do you have another coat of arms with the same banner on the cape? "Alice says

"Yes I have many in a lot of other rooms." Michael says

"Get one that matches this one as close as you can "Alice says

5:37 pm

Alice stands fully decked out in the battle armor with her green cape draping

In the back. There is no helmet with this suit it was issued this way Alice still feels light as a feather

She should feel a little weight from the new attire but her strength is 20 times what a normal human is Michael comes in the room in his matching battle armor

With his matching golden lion symbol on his cape

"We'll pass for Royal Knights "Alice says

"You just let me do the talking you just nod yes or no do not speak "Alice says

"So you think this plan will work?" Michael says

"It's our best shot "Alice says

"Let's armor the horses and be on our way "Alice says

6:00 pm the streets of Transylvania

Alice and Michael ride out of the village quickly no one even sees them. They ride over the mountains to the north. The way they are dressed they do look like knights this plan just

Might work. They ride until 10:55pm then they stop and tie their horses and take off their

Battle armor and wait for the moon. They are only an hour away from the castle. The Moon starts to come out

"This is it Michael I'll see you back here tomorrow "Alice says

"Unless we get killed during the night." Michael says

"No one knows how to kill us yet Michael we will be fine. I just hope nobody gets in our way "Alice says

"OH God I can feel it coming "Alice says

The two fall to their knees and the transformation begins

O H Go D Ahooooooooooooll!!!!

The two wolfs run up the mountain side one following the other. You can hear two howls off in the distance AHOOOOL!!! AHOOOL!!!!

8:08 AM TUE SEP 1575 AN HOUR AWAY FROM THE CASTLE

Alice and Michael have made it back to the spot where their

horses

Was tied they have gotten back into their battle armor they are always a little weak just after

Transforming back but it will wear off in an hour.

Alice goes to her saddle bag on her horse she gets the light pistol .she puts it in her inside pocket of her steal knitted shirt

They mount their horses and start to make their way to the castle

they arrive at the castle at 9:15 am .it's a huge structure frost thinks to herself the castle is probably 300 years old they ride up to the draw bridge Alice yells   "Royal knights with business here "Alice says in a commanding voice .A few moments pass they hear no one

Then slowly the steal gate door begins to raise

"Ok Michael we are on "Alice says whispering

The two ride through the door way were the metal gate raised

A servant comes there way they get off their horses

there is no way of knowing if the strain of virus will completely stop them from transforming is unclear to Alice   she has already started thinking ahead wondering if she can survive as a vampire on

 Animal blood Alice is thinking of saving lives and if this plan works the werewolf virus could be

 wiped out on this planet Alice is planning on saving a sample of her blood in the future for all she knows that's where modern medicine

 Comes from she has no intentions of killing this Drake if her plan works she hopes this strain of virus will not change you as

 Who you are as a person she plans on studying this man to determine if it will Alice thinks to

 Herself this man probably thinks he's sick because he can't go into the sunlight so the less he

Knows the better .The served grabs their horses

"suntem cavaleri regale de investigare atacurile care sa întâmplat ne-ar dori să vorbească

 cu numărul de"."We are royal knights investigating the attacks that's been happening we

 Would like to speak to Drake" Alice says to the servant

"Void lua caii""I will take your horses" the servant says

The two walk up to a giant wooden door. "Ok Michael follow my lead say as little as you

 Can let me do the talking" Alice says

"Knock on the Door "Alice says

Michael grabs the metal circle that knocks the door he knocks it several times

Seconds pass

The door opens .it's another servant

"da"Yes" The servant says

"suntem cavaleri regale de investigare atacurile care sa întâmplat ne-ar dori să vorbească

 cu numărul de"."We are royal knights investigating the attacks that's been happening we

 Would like to speak to Drake" Alice says to the servant

"vin in i se va informa numărul de" "come in i will inform him" The Door Man Says

The two walk in. all the curtains were pulled closed there was only candle light it was well

 Decorated with many expensive things there was a huge fire place in the center of the room

There was a fire in the hearth Alice walks to the fire place which was as tall as she was she still'

Can't believe whose fire she's standing in front of they hear a voice from beside them

 Coming toward them

"What do royal Knights care of a few murders in Transylvania? "The voice says

"You speak English. That's well" Alice says turning toward the voice

"Yes I Know of England" he says

"We are investigating a string of murders just like these all up and down the country side when

We heard you was attacked and survived we wanted to talk to you"

"I can't tell you a thing I was so sick I was knocked out the moment I came off my horse"

"You seem to have recovered very quickly Drake "Alice says

"Yes I Am a Very Lucky Man "he says

"we came here hoping to get a sample of your blood we believe it contains clues about the creature"

"Yes I will do whatever I can to help "he says

Alice pulls out a glass vial that she got from Michaels Home

"If you can fill this we will be on our way "Alice says

Alice draws her sword "if you will hold your hand out I'll make this as painless has I can" Alice says

He holds his right hand out and Alice Swipes her blade across the palm blood pours

Alice puts the glass vial which is a large one at the base of the wound .she catches the precious

Blood it fills the vial quickly by the time the vial is full the wound on the hand had

Already held shut. Alice looks at Drake. She decides to give him a little information

He seemed like a good man he's just as innocent as Alice was herself in all of this

"It's a side effect from you being infected by this creature that's why your wounds heal instantly

And you're allergic to the sun. Can I see your teeth?"

 He looks as if he doesn't want to show her but he does .Alice looks at his fangs which are

 Just an inch and a half longer than her own teeth they looked razor sharp

Alice puts the cork on the glass vial of blood and puts it in her pocket

"Have you eaten anything since the attack "Alice ask

"I Tried to eat but I got sick when I tried it's so strange I have not eaten in two days but I am not even hungry" Drake Says

"Your blood has been infected by this creature that attacked you your body is not going

 To crave food anymore it will crave blood I suggest you fill your corals with livestock and try that

 Blood you seem like a good man you don't want to become a monster"

He looks shocked

"Will you do me a favor will you keep my name out of your report to your superiors"

"Don't worry we are not after you but your name will be left out"

"Tell me have you noticed any other side effects that you have been experiencing"

"This is the strangest thing that's ever happened to me last night I was in my tower in my library

I had a thought I would go down to the cellar and see if I could drink some wine but the

Moment I thought about the cellar I appeared in the cellar the door to the cellar was still locked

I had to get a servant to let me out .do you think this is a side effect" he says

"Everything that happens to you from this point when you was attacked is a side effect .I was

Going to deny you this information but I'm hoping it will save lives that's why I'm telling you I

Came here expecting to have to kill you but your just as innocent as the next try to stay that

Way .we will be on our way now. Until we meet again on another day "I didn't even get your name" he says

"It's Alice Frost" she says

"Then so Long Alice" Drake says with his Transylvania accent

Alice and Michael walk out the door the served closes it AS they leave. Their horses are waiting

On them outside they mount their horses and ride back out the gate they came through. Alice

Looks at Michael

"That went extremely well I was expecting a war "Alice says to Michael

"Did you see how pale he was Alice? "Michael Asks

"I'll be pale if it means I won't turn into a werewolf ever time the moon comes out it's still early

We might make it back to your home before it gets dark we will drink the blood there "Alice

Says

The two ride hard all day and into the late evening its 7:32 pm when they arrive at Michaels

 Home they put their horses up and walk into Michael home the moon will be out in mines

If this doesn't work they will transform into a werewolf in the village Michael brings fire from the

 Hearth and lights the torches attached to the walls Alice takes her battle armor off she has her

 Other clothes on underneath her lays the vial of blood and the light pistol down on a desk

Michael comes in the room he is still wearing his armor Alice grabs the vial of blood

"Here Michael you go first drink some of this "Alice says to Michael

 Takes the lid off the vial and hands it to Michael the brave he drinks a big drink of it and hands it to

Alice she takes a big drink of it there's still a good bit of blood left in the vial Michael puts the top

Back on it and lays it back down on the desk. She feels a warm feeling in her stomach she looks

At Michael the color leaves his face his eyes turn from brown to light blue Alice feels for her

Pulse she can't find one they go outside the moon is coming out just over the trees

"It worked Alice we are not going to change" Michael says

"Yes Michael the werewolf virus is gone "Alice says

But the werewolf versus was very much still alive there had been attacks on their very last

 Transformation and there was a survivor who is changing into a werewolf this very moment

Alice Frost Helped Michael Fake his death on the morning of august the 09 1601

. Alice and Michael

Live haply as vampires for the next 300 years the story continues in 1875

.................Until 1875 I leave you to these writings..........

Time trip 1875 chapter five

By

Jase Watkins

JAN 2 1875 Transylvania

It was a cold bitter night in Transylvania it was 10:32 PM and it was snowing hard

There was already a foot of snow covering everything .If you was a human or had any

Brains in your head you was in front of a fire somewhere warm but there was something

About to happen on one of the side streets of Transylvania which had grew in size in

Three hundred years.

 Transylvania had become a hot spot for werewolf and vampire hunters

They would come from all over the world with two things on their mind killing either a

 Werewolf

Or a vampire .thinking their trophy of a werewolf or a vampire will make them famous.

But there's a problem with thinking like this the problem is there never would be a trophy of a

Werewolf or a vampire because all you have left after you kill both is either a pill of ashes or a

Nude dead human with a silver bullet lodged in its heart or where ever you was lucky enough

To shoot one at. Years back there had even been a hunter kill an innocent women claiming she

Was a vampire. This women's family tracked this hunter down brought him back to Transylvania

And hung him. But the bounty hunters keep coming every year more and more walk the streets

And forest of Transylvania. .One was walking down a side street on this bitter cold night he was

Following a young women dressed in a black robe and hood he suspected her to be a vampire

Since she was the only other person out in this weather. She is about fifty feet ahead of him he

Starts to walk faster to catch up with her at the same time she slows down. The hunter has A

Large cross in his left hand his belt has three loops on the side and there's wooden stakes in the

Loops just as a gunfighter would wear his bullets on his belt. As he gets closer he pulls out one

Of the stakes with his right hand he taps the lady on the shoulder with the stake. She stops

Walking.

"Turn around" The Hunter says aggressively

The women turns around slowly her face can't be seen because of the hooded robe she is

Wearing. The Hunter holds the cross up

"Touch the cross now" The hunter says to the women

"You Mean like this" the women says reaching out and grasping the cross

The man shakes his head in disappointment he puts the stake back in its loop

"Now I must ask you for something" The women says

"I have no money for a beggar" The hunter says

"Oh it's not your money I want.....ITS YOUR BLOOD!!!!

The hooded figure springs onto the hunter in a blink of an eye going for his neck

The hunter falls dead to the street within a few moments

The women removes her hood

It was Alice. She hadn't aged a day in 300 years

"Silly fool you believed everything you ever read about vampires" Alice says to the dead

 Vampire hunter

She takes the cross from the dead man's hand

"This is a nice one it will fit right in with my collection now to dispose of you where

 You'll be out of everyone's way" Alice Says

Reaching down with one hand she lifts the dead body and throws it over her shoulder

 Alice

Vanishes with the body into thin air .Deep in the forest overlooking a bluff Alice appears

 Out of nowhere

She throws the body over the bluff seconds pass she hears it smack into rocks at the

 Bottom of

The bluff

"Well if I didn't kill you that sure as hell did" Alice says to herself

Alice surely did not drink human blood but she does whenever she kills one of these

Bounty hunters who was being stalked the whole time by Alice from the front

She vanishes from the side of the bluff and reappears back on the street where she was

 Originally

At. She pulls her hood over her head again she wasn't cold she hears someone coming by

Horse

She wasn't really worried or scared from the people of Transylvania a few of them even

Knew she

Was a vampire but they didn't look at Alice as a threat the ones who knew she was a

Vampire

They knew she lived off the blood of animals she even has a human friend who wants Alice to

Turn her

Into a vampire but Alice refuses every time the subject comes up because Alice says the

Girl is

Too young to become a vampire at just 19 years old this girl has become a very dear friend

To Alice with Michael leaving Transylvania 50 years ago he went on a visit to New York

And met

A young women there and fell in love and had stayed Alice was heartbroken they was

Never

Together but after knowing him for century's she had feelings for him she was planning on

Telling

Him when he returned from his trip but he never came back Alice got a letter from him a

Year

After he left explaining that he had met the love of his life she still gets letters from him

From time to time but he's happy with this women he even turned her so they will

Probably always be together Michael had originally went to New York to see the town Alice has regretted it

Ever since. The horse and rider pass by Alice on the street the rider pays her no mind.

Alice was in the newest part of Transylvania none of this was here

300 years ago when she

Arrived .Alice walks on down the street. She hears a girl crying and sobbing. Another

Broken heart Alice says to herself. She spots the girl two hundred yards up the street

Coming her way it was Laminate her human friend that wants to be a vampire. Alice

Travels the two hundred yards in under a second

"Laminate what's the matter why are you crying "Alice Ask

Laminate sees Alice and grabs her and hugs her crying even harder

Alice Grabs Laminate by the shoulders and looks into her face her eye was

Bruised. "Laminate who has hit you?" Alice ask angel

Laminate just hugs Alice again and cry's more

"Come on Laminate I'll Walk You Home"

"C a Can't Go home Right now Alice" Laminate says crying

"Did Your Father do this" Alice ask concerned

"He does not mean Alice" Luminita says still crying

"Come I Will Have a Talk with him" Alice says in a demanding voice

"Will make worse Alice No" Laminate says

"Well you can't stay out much longer it's below freezing "Alice says in a concerned voice

"Come on Laminate you can stay with me tonight I was just heading in myself" Alice says

Laminate hugs Alice again this time with less crying

"Your Good friend Alice" Laminate says with even less crying

Laminate turns and starts walking in the direction Alice was walking

Alice picks up the pace she senses that Laminate almost has frost bite

The two make it to Alice's place in under ten mines Alice still lived in Michaels

Home. In one of his letters to Michael He had given her the home

The two go inside. Alice kept a fire going at all times to light the torches on the wall

"Go stand in front of the fire Laminate" Alice says

Laminate dosses trembling all over

"How long have you been outside today Laminate? "Alice ask

"A All Day" Luminita says trembling

"Do YOU Want Die or something" Alice says

"Yes I Do... Want to be like you" Luminita says still shivering

"Not Now Luminita" Alice says sharply

"When then?" Luminita ask

"Luminita I mean this is not a good time to talk about that" Alice
says

"Is this the first time your father has hit you?" Alice Ask

"Not first time." Luminita says

"How long has this been going on?" Alice Asks

"Since I was small. After my mother died it got worse." Luminita
says with tears beginning
 To tear up in her eyes

"He is the only family you have left?" Alice ask

"Yesses" Luminita says breaking out crying again

"Don't Cry Luminita you can stay here with me I haven't seen my
family in 300 years I

Know what it's like to feel like you're alone and I have changed my mind and if you still

Want to be what I Am Then I will give it to you" Alice says with a most serious tone to her

Voice

Laminate stops crying and has the strangest look on her face almost a look of over joyous

Luminita was a little taller than Alice about 5'11 in height with bright red hair and

Green eyes Alice was sitting on a cushion padded double size arm chair they are about ten

Feet apart from each other

Alice takes her pointing finger and moves it back and forth signaling Luminita to come

To her

"Come sit with me Luminita I don't bite....Hard

Luminita quickly starts to move toward Alice she sits down in the chair made for two next

To Alice

"You're A Very Beautiful Girl Luminita" Alice says softly

Alice strokes Luminita hair

"You're So Beautiful sweaty you would have beautiful children and a family of your own

 Someday are you really sure this is what you want" Alice says

"Want more than anything Alice "Luminita says desperately

Luminita is staring into Alice's eyes

"I want you to make me like you "Luminita says

Alice stands up pulling Luminita to her feet too

And moves her mouth to Laminate's neck "Are You Ready Luminita." Alice says

In a whisper "Am Ready "Luminita says trembling

Alice aggressively sinks her fangs into Luminita

I I ii I I I I I "Luminita moans even more

The moment the Blood enters Alice' mouth her eyes widen it was the sweetest blood

Alice has ever tasted. She drinks for a few seconds more than pushes Luminita away from

Her

Alice Looks at Laminate's face she sees the bruise on Laminate's eye disappear the color

Leaves from her face her beautiful green eyes change color

"You're a vampire how does it feel" Alice ask smiling

The two puncher wounds on Luminita neck still have some blood coming out

Luminita takes her fingers and feels of her two newly grown fangs

"Feels like nothing have felt before "Luminita says with an accent

Alice sees the blood coming out of the wounds on Luminita neck

Alice looks at the master clock its 12:07 Pm

"Get Dressed Luminita I'm Taking you out we have to close the wounds on your neck"
 Alice says

"Now look into my eyes Luminita and don't look away "Alice Says

Luminita looks into Alice's eyes the room starts to spin she closes her eyes to try and

Stop from spinning when she opens them her and Alice are standing in the middle of

The forest

"Where are we Alice?" Luminita ask

"Three Hours away from Transylvania there is a large herd of deer bedded down just over

The hill you need to drink blood to close those wounds wait right here "Alice says

Alice disappears into thin air a few moments later Luminita hears a deer bleating it sounds

Terrified

Alice reappears in front of Luminita holding a small female deer it was kicking and still

Making a god awful noise that was hurting Luminita new Vampire ears

Alice pulls the hair out on a spot on the deer's neck

"Hurry and drink Luminita before this dam thing attracts a werewolf "Alice says

Luminita can smell the blood inside of the animal .instincts take over Luminita

Sinks her new Vampire Vans into the bald spot on the neck of the animal blood pours

Into Luminita Mouth her eyes widen she begins to swallow the blood Luminita drinks

The blood for a full two Minutes

"That's enough Luminita it will make you sick the first time if you drink too much" Alice

Says

Alice drops the lifeless body of the dead animal. She pushes Luminita head around so

She can get a good look at her neck. The wounds had already healed

"How do you feel Luminita? "Alice Ask

"Like never feel before Alice "Luminita says in an excited tone

To a vampire blood of any kind is like a narcotic drug to them the high last for about

Six hours human blood is the most potent but if Alice and Luminita start feeding

On humans it would eventually bring unwanted attention their way and Alice survives

By keeping a low profile it was the vampires Drake created that caused all the

Problems .he had left Romania 100 years after he was visited by Alice

But there was many powerful vampires some as old as Alice left scattered throughout

Romania some close by A few even knew of Alice but only two people knew what a

Vampire really was which a mutated strain of virus was originating from a distant planet

And that Alice who had been an astronaut and Commander of this failed mission

Arrived back on earth in the year 1575 crashing into the sea and she ends up in

Transylvania carrying the original werewolf virus and had become a vampire by tricking

Drake into giving her a sample of his blood which had

Been invested by Alice herself as a werewolf... Alice later learned that the count had been

Sick with a virus and that that's what caused the mutation of the werewolf virus and that

Alice was Even More Powerful than the Him. Alice Knows this And Michael knows

This. Alice Had decided not to share this information with Luminita

She trust her but if some of this information was known every bounty hunter werewolf

Hunter and vampire hunter in the world would be coming for Alice

Alice Knew she would have to leave Romania someday the only people that know she's a

Vampire are close friends 4 people including Luminita and Michael the other two was

People she help out in the forest when they was almost attacked by a werewolf it was

Five years ago so these other two people are not going to betray the person they owe their

Life to .Alice had leaped at incredible speed at the werewolf And Decapitated it. She explained to these two people that she lives off of

Animal blood and they agreed to never tell a soul

"Ok Luminita I'm Going to teach you something I want you to think of my fire place

 Picture yourself standing in front of it feel the warmth from the fire close your eyes

    The moment Luminita closed her eyes she vanished into thin air

    "I Feel fire Alice I can feel it "Luminita says

    She opens her eyes she's standing in front of the fire at Alice's Home

    "Alice "Luminita says

But it's just Luminita standing in front of the fire

Alice Appears out of thin air at the side of the fire

"Alice I liked That Trick "Luminita says

"Comes in handy for a quick trip to the fridge" Alice Says
Smiling

"Alice What Is Fridge?" Luminita Ask with innocence

Alice smiles "The Food Is There" Alice Says

Luminita was still feeling the effect from the blood she drank

For a human it would feel like overdosing on morphine

But a vampire will never overdose on blood. A new vampire
might get sick

The first time they drink if they drink too much but it's nothing
serious

Luminita would not get sick she's as high as a kite from this heroin like food

Substances she must consume at least 3 times a week

"Come Luminita lets pick you out a bedroom" Alice says

"See the balcony above us use the trick like I showed you to appear there" Alice says

Luminita disappears and reappears on the upper level of the house Alice is right behind her

The two go down the hallway with many doors Luminita goes into one of the rooms

There was porcelain torches with fuel inside the porcelain cup and was burning producing

A great deal of light the room Luminita goes in is nice with a very elaborate bed the bed

It was two hundred years old but it's a very good one and rather expensive Luminita

Was from much poorer conditions this room more than suited her

"Where's your room Alice? "Luminita ask

"Just down the hall" Alice says

"Ok I'll Pick This Room Alice "Luminita says

"This use to be my room you'll like the bed I promise you, the sun comes up in four hours

I have some business I have to take care of in another part of the country for now do not leave

The house but explore it I have many fine clothes most will fit you play dress up......but do not leave

This house all the doors are latched shut open them for no one but me but I never use the door "Alice Explains

"Alice when will you return and why can't I come? "Luminita ask

"I'll Be Back Before the sun comes the people I'm seeing tonight does not like new people this

 Will be my last meeting with these people there would be nothing to do Luminita "Alice says

"Ok Alice will be here "Luminita says With Accent

"Remember do not leave this house "Alice says

"Will not leave Alice" Luminita says

Alice disappears out of the room and reappears in her own room she opens a cabinet she pulls

Out a rolled up cloth she unwraps the cloth...it's the light pistol she puts it in a pocket in her robe

And disappears again this time she reappears all the way across Romania at a harbor by the bay

A large ship the style of the day sit in the bay it had its sails down and was anchored

 Inside the

Local tavern two generals from the army a congressmen from Washington DC and a dozen

Soldiers sit almost asleep at the bar they awaken as Alice Frost opens the door she steps in

Miss Do you know how long we have been waiting for you?" the congressmen says

 Getting out of his seat.

"I'm sorry I'm late do you have the money?" Alice ask

"Yes we had to make half of it but its 50 million in 20 dollar gold coins the two generals

That brought it would like to see the same test of the weapon that you showed me"

"Let's go through the back out the back door of this place in the back behind the building" Alice says

The congressmen and the two generals and five of the soldiers and Alice went out back

Behind the bar

They all gather just outside the back door 2 of the soldiers have a brown leather duffle bag

In the bag was 50 million in mostly brand new 20 dolor gold pieces the bag was laying on

The ground it was too heavy to stand and hold

"Ok we have come very far and this is a lot of money this weapon better be worth it

And it better do what was claimed of it:" one of the Generals says in a commanding voice

Alice pulls from her pocket the silver metallic light weapon that was issued to Alice in the

Year 2058 she hands it to one of the generals he inspects the weapon

"It doesn't look like much" The General says as he hands the weapon to the other general

"Ok let's see what this thing can do" the second general holding the light pistol says

Handing the pistol to Alice

She takes the pistol. "Ok Gentlemen you see that large boulder 50 feet over there" Alice

Says pointing at a large rock sitting off in the distance

They all shake their head and say they see the rock

Alice draws a bead on the large boulder she pulls the trigger

A blueish white light ball fly's from the pistol at great speed striking

The boulder. In a fraction of a second the boulder explodes into several

Red hot melted chunks of smaller rock

"Wow!" One of the generals says

"I want to fire it once "The other general says

Alice explains there is a security feature in the weapon and it will only fire in her

Hands at the moment.

"I Suggest you put your best people on studying this weapon someday you will be able

To produce ones just like it" Alice says to the general that wanted to fire the weapon

One of the Generals motions for the soldiers guarding the duffle bag of 20 dollar gold

Coins. "Give her the money" one general says

They drop the heavy bag at the feet of Alice she hands the weapon to one of the

Generals he takes it

"What country has developed this weapon" the general ask Alice as he takes the weapon

Of the future from Alice

"It was developed by a single man he's dead this is the only prototype if you don't

Developed this weapon it will never exist" Alice says reaching down acting like the bag is

Heavy as she picks it up easily

"Miss you have done a great thing for the sake of your country" the general says

Handing the pistol to the other general

"You Have no Idea Gentlemen. I must be on my way now it was a pleasure doing

 Business with you "Alice says turning walking back through the bar she disappears

The moment she enters the back of the bar and she is out of sight she reappears back

In her home in Transylvania in front of the fire place Luminita didn't see Alice yet

She was dressed up in battle armor playing in the corner of the room with a sword

"Luminita I like your Battle armor "Alice says laughing

A Startled Luminita looks in Alice's Direction

"Alice you are back. Hats in the bag? "Luminita ask curiously

"Our Nest Egg" Alice says

She throws the bag to Luminita who catches it with ease

"These are heavy Eggs Alice" Luminita says

Alice smiles

"Look in The bag Luminita "Alice says taking her outer robe off and lays it on a chair

Luminita looks in the bag

Her eyes sparkle at what she sees she reaches in and grabs a hand full of Gold coins

"Alice how did you get all of this" Luminita ask rubbing her hands all in the bag

Of gold coins

"I Sold some real estate in America that I owned" Alice says lying out her teeth

"How Much Is Here "Luminita ask

"50 Million American "Alice says

"Alice this is lot of money you are the richest person in Romania" Luminita says dropping

Coins back in the bag one at a time

"Come let's put it up I already have money here in the safe this money is savings

For the future .someday each coin will be worth thousands of American dollars for each

And every single one of these" Alice says to Luminita

They walk out of the main giant room into an office where the giant wall safe was at

Luminita is carrying the bag of 20 dollar gold coins. Alice swings a painting open from

The wall and reveals a large wall safe it's huge Alice puts in the combinations on the safe

She opens it with the latch on the safe it was filled with gold large bills of Romanian

Money there was jewels ruby's satires diamonds most of which was in the safe when

Alice arrived here 300 years ago. Alice motions for Luminita to throw her the bag. She

Does .Alice catches the heavy bag of gold coins with ease she puts it in the back of the

Safe. Alice grabs a ruby neckless from the safe she tosses it to Luminita

"Some jewels for you to wear you never worn jewels before have you Luminita" Alice ask

"No Have not it is beautiful Alice "Luminita says holding the jeweled necklace up to her

Neck looking at herself in the mirror that was in the office.

"Did you look in your closet in your room?" Alice ask Luminita

"No did not "Luminita says

"It's full of some really nice clothes you can have everything that fits you "Alice says

"I Go Look "Luminita Says disappearing into thin air

Alice smiles and closes the safe and the painting

Alice hears the battle Armor being dropped on the floor in Luminita room

"I bet she puts on the red dress "Alice says to herself in a whisper

Alice leans up against the desk that was in the office waiting on Luminita to

Come back in the room showing herself off in a fancy dress and Alice knew

She would want her to put the ruby jeweled necklace on her

A Few moments pass then Luminita reappears in the office with Alice

She is wearing the very dress Alice said she would put on

"You Look Very nice Luminita "Alice says

Luminita hands the rubies to Alice and ask her to put them on her

Alice takes the rubies from Luminita

"Turn around" Alice says

Alice puts the necklace on Luminita from behind and fastens the latch on the necklace

"There you go" Alice says

Luminita stands in front of the mirror looking at her reflection that she was not supposed

Have. She reaches up and touches her necklace Alice is standing across the room with her

Head pop through the thick triple layered curtains looking out the window at the sky

Becoming brighter. The sun will be hitting the windows in 15 mines Alice brings her head

Back out from the thick specially made curtains closes them fully she looked at the bed

Most vampires can't keep their home secure but they had designed sophisticated metal

Boxes they could only be opened from the inside. They could guarantee that no stake

Would find its way in its heart while the vampire slept and that they could not be burned

Alive during the day by an intruder. Alice has two of these custom made boxes they was

In a secret passage behind through one of the medium size fire places there was never a fire

In this hearth it's in a large room with no windows this was one of the oldest homes

In Transylvania it was six hundred years older than Alice it was originally built by a very

Wealthy knight this secret passage is one of many and is the equivalent to the modern

Day safe room but Alice's Home is as securer than any its doors and locks were built

With military technology of the day Alice's home was one huge coffin. But Alice plans

On showing Luminita this safe room behind the secret passage way through the fire place

In one of the larger rooms when they awake tonight no one would ever find them in case

Of an emergency the way it was opened there was a small stone button on the floor all the

Way on the other side of the room in the corner the floors was made out of granite tiles the

Home looked like a normal home but underneath the other layer the home was built out of

The same material the castles are built from it was a secret castle the knight that built it

Had access to the best military structure designs from England. Alice knew every secret

That this large structure held it's been her safe haven for 300 years

Alice had been staring at the bed for five mines .she was thinking of Michael she looks at

Luminita who is still looking at her necklace the sun will be up in 10 mines

Luminita walks away from the mirror all dressed up looking like she just came from a

Fancy party she gets a little closer to Alice about ten feet apart now

"What you thinking Alice?"

"Just of someone I Knew" Alice Says

'The Sun will be up in a few mines stay away from the windows try and get some sleep

We will catch another deer when we wake goodnight Luminita "Alice Says

Alice disappears as soon as she closed her eyes

"Goodnight Alice" Luminita says standing alone now

Luminita goes to the window which all had extremely thick glass which someday

Would be used as safety glass in cars of modern times some ancient military technology

From England even a bullet from a high powered rifle could not penetrate it there would

Never be a fire bomb thrown through the windows the home was tighter than a bank fault

Luminita peeks through the triple thick layer curtains the sky is light now but the suns not over the

Mountains yet it will be fully over the mountains in 8 mines Luminita changes into some

Sleeping clothes and gets into the luxury bed made in France she falls asleep within

Mines Alice is in her room it's the master bedroom of the house it's very large with a giant

Office desk in the corner Alice's Bed Was Even More elaborate Than Luminita it had

A draped white silk veil hood covering the bed reaching all the way to the floor Alice sit

At her desk there is a lap on the desk burning lantern fuel she is writing in her journal

Alice had kept it ever since she had become a vampire it was a very large book it contained

Day to day events that has happened to Alice for the last 300 years
she closes the book

Walks to the window and looks through the same type curtains that
was made just to keep

The sunlight out the edge of the sun is starting to break over the
mountains she close the

Curtain Alice dress in a sleeping robe pushes the silk drapes apart on
her bed and gets in it

She always leaves the lamp burning Alice is Asleep within Mines
.The two vampires Will

Sleep until the Sun is down over on the other side of the
mountains....................The Story

Continues On Jan 3 1875 at 6:58 PM

Time Trip Chapter Six 1875

By

Jase Watkins

Alice opens her eyes she pushes the Silk Drapes Back And gets out of her bed

She goes to the walk in closet there was clothes on both side 20 feet back into the wall

She grabs a dressier outfit than her black robe she was wearing last night

She puts on a cream shirt she put on tight black pants she had on a short

Fitting red jacket with black trim Alice puts her knee high leather boots on them were skin

Tight on Alice and gave her good footing Alice disappears from her room and reappears in the

Room that has the fire in the fire place she looks at the master clock its 7:05Pm She Walks

Over to the giant window in the room she pops her head through the curtains she can see the

Mountains that the sun sets behind the sun had been down for only a few mines it was still

Light outside Alice would always Love to go outside and walk the streets this wishing hour as she

Called it because it's the hour a day that she can go out in the daylight and she always wishes

It would stay like this for a while longer. Alice had put on a much nicer wardrobe because she

planed on taking Luminita to Budapest in Hungary Tonight she owned a nice home on by the

Water side there Alice knew she would have to help Luminita Get there because she had

Never left Transylvania but Alice can help her appear there with her... Alice had a few Bottles

Of Blood stored in the Home in Budapest Luminita Was the first Vampire Alice as Ever created

She was happy with her decision to make her a Vampire Knowing she will have a longer

And better life would never go without something to eat and as long as Alice was around

Would be safe from harm. Alice Appears outside on a back street back in the bushes she steps

Out

From the bushes no one was watching her there's about 37 mines of light left Alice walked the

Streets of Transylvania For the next 37 mines she even saw one of the friends that she saved

From a werewolf one night five years ago it was friendly hellos and goodbyes with a great deal

Of respect paid to Alice .The light had failed and now it was dark Alice Vanishes from a side

Street she was on and appears in Luminita room at the side of her bed Luminita was still

Asleep Alice puts her hand on Luminita forehead she had a normal temperature of a

Vampire she was a little cooler than a human was. Luminita opened her eyes as Alice

Removed her hand from her forehead

"Sleep well Luminita" Alice Ask

"Yes Sleep well Alice" Luminita says raising up in bed

"Find something nice to wear I'm Taking you to Budapest Tonight" Alice Says walking to the closet door

"Budapest" Luminita says excitedly

"Yes it's very beautiful there I want to show you a few places" Alice says opening the closet door

Alice grabs several outfits that she think might fit Luminita and lay them on her bed

Luminita gets out of bed and picks out the outfit she wants to wear it's an all-black

Outfit tight pants and jacket similar to the one Alice has on

"We Will get you some boots in one of the shops in Budapest for now wear your old ones" Alice says

Luminita Takes the bed clothes off she is wearing and changes into her outfit

"How Long You Been Wake Alice" Luminita ask fastening the latches on her shirt

"Not Long" Alice Says

Luminita stand fully clothed in very expensive clothes the outfit she has on now cost

More than her old house would cost to build today. Luminita says she is hungry

"We Will Drink before we go to Budapest" Alice says

"Remember the forest picture yourself in that same spot and close your eyes Alice says

Luminita close her eyes and disappears Alice Disappears and appears in the forest standing

Next to Luminita

"I'll see if they are still bedded down they surely still are here at this time "Alice says Whispering

Alice Disappears and in a few moments Luminita Hears a Deer Being Caught by Alice

Alice reappears in Front Of Luminita Holding a Kicking and Screaming Young Deer

Alice Pulls the Hair out Of the Deer's Neck

"Go Ahead Luminita you drink from this one. Luminta takes the deer from Alice And

Sinks Her Fangs into the Deer She Drinks Until No More Blood Is
Coming Out

Alice disappears again this time Luminita Hears another deer further
out in the distance

Being caught .Alice reappears with another Small Deer She Pulls the
Hair from Its Neck

She Sinks Her Fangs into the Animal Witch Give a Loud Blade but
Makes No More Noise

As The Blood Is Slow Drain from the Creature

Luminita Stood Watching Alice Drink the Blood She Had Dropped
Her Deer On The

Forest Floor

Alice Finishes Hers She Had been on her Knees Holding the animal
she stands up

Holding her deer

"Grab Your Deer Luminita "Alice says

Now Look into My Eyes.....Luminita Holds the dead animal looks into Alice Eyes

The forest starts to spin she closed her eyes when she opens them she's standing

In Front of a small home in the forest Alice is next to her holding her deer

Alice Lays the Dead Animal on the Porch of the Old Home

"Lay it Down over Here Luminita" Alice Points right next to the dead deer laying

On the porch

Luminita lays it down

"An 80 Year Old Lady Lives Here I leave her most of the animals I kill "Alice says

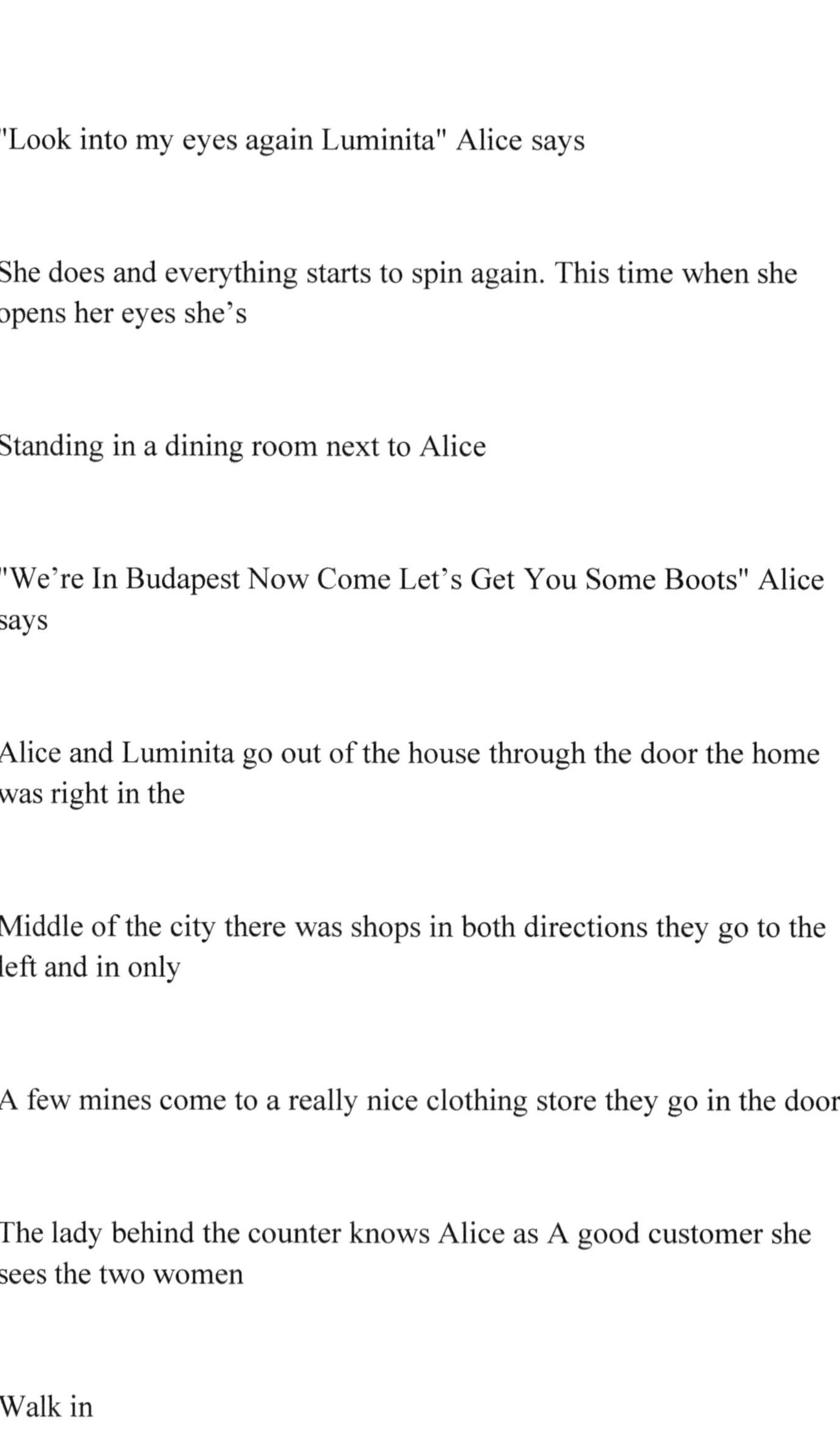

"Look into my eyes again Luminita" Alice says

She does and everything starts to spin again. This time when she opens her eyes she's

Standing in a dining room next to Alice

"We're In Budapest Now Come Let's Get You Some Boots" Alice says

Alice and Luminita go out of the house through the door the home was right in the

Middle of the city there was shops in both directions they go to the left and in only

A few mines come to a really nice clothing store they go in the door

The lady behind the counter knows Alice as A good customer she sees the two women

Walk in

"Miss it's Good to See You Again "The Lady says to Alice with an Accent

"Hello We Are Here For Boots Something Similar to the ones I'm Wearing" Alice Says

What Size" The Lady Ask

Luminita Tells the Lady What Size Shoe She Thinks She Can Wear

"Have Just the Pair Wait Here "The Lady Says Going into a Back Room

She Brings a Box Out with her and opens it." These are very comfortable" The women says

Luminita Puts Them on "I Like" Luminita says

Alice Played the Lady with Cash

The two start to walk out of the shop

The Lady Says "Do You Want Your Old Shoes"

Alice knew this lady was involved with charities for the needy Alice tells her to

Donate them to the poor. The Two Vampires Walk Out Of the Shop

The Two Walk by one of the Castles of Budapest Luminita Marvels at its size

And Beauty

"Come on Luminita I'm Taking You to one of the Palace Hotels for a Drink and they

 Have heated pools of water it will feel most good on this cold night "Alice says

"Alice I didn't think Vampires could drink Alcohol I don't think I want any" Luminita says

"It's Not Alcohol and trust me you'll want this drink "Alice says

"Come On" Alice says again

Luminita starts walking again they walk for about 15 mines taking their time taking in the

City with all its beauty they come to one of the older nicer Palace Hotels and They Enter

The Well Lite Structure Through the front doors which is opened for them by a door man

"This Way Luminita "Alice says

She follows Alice into the recreant part of the hotel

Alice tells the Hastiest that she would like her regular table and waiter

The Young women Leads the two Vampires to the center Table in the Dining Area

Which is almost packed they sit down their two menus on the table. Luminita is looking

Around the room and at all the strange faces

"Come Here Allot Alice "Luminita Ask

"Mabey 10 Times in the Last Five Years" Alice Says

A Male waiter comes to the table he knows Alice

"Alice it's good to Finally See You Again" The Waiter says in a
friendly voice

"Thanks Rafael It's good To See you too bring us two Glasses"
Alice says looking into

 The eyes of the young waiter

"Bring right out Alice" Rafael Says leavening their table heading for
the back room

The waiter comes back carrying a green bottle and two wine glasses
he sits the Glasses down on

Table One In Front of each of the women he removes the cork from the bottle he pours

Each of their wine glasses full Puts the cork back on the bottle then ask

"Anything else Alice" The young waiter says

Rafael we will be finishing these drinks in one of the smaller heated pools can you bring

Us two bathing suits

"Anything for you Alice" Rafael says

He leaves the table Luminita smells of the red liquid in her Glass

"This is Blood" Luminita says Amazed

"The Waiter Is a Vampire Its Rabbit Blood the most potent of all animal blood it's sold on the black market to

Vampires All across the Region No One Dies from Us Drinking This Blood So There's

No Pressure for It to Stop Try Not To Get Addicted To It May Not Always Be

Around Have a Taste" Alice Says

Luminita Takes A Drink of the Blood It Taste Sweet as Sugar and Moments After the

Blood Touches Luminita Stomach She Gets a High Similar to the effects Heroin And

Cocaine Has on Humans Luminita closes her eyes as she takes another sip she feels

Another massive rush of energy flush all parts of her body

"Drink Slowly Luminita it can overcome you the first time you drink it if you drink to fast" Alice says taking a sip from her own glass

"Alice what is bathing suit?" Luminita ask

"It's something to wear in the water" Alice says

Luminita hadn't been swimming since three summers ago she was
excited about that

She had never wore a bathing suit or had even heard of such a thing
she would always swim nude

"Luminita you're going to collage someday when they start opening
24 hours a day you'll love it" Alice says

"Alice what is Collage "Luminita ask

"School you learn things there that place you stopped going when
you was eight"

Luminita had very few skills when it came to reading and writing
Alice had thought

She to speak English over the years she had knew her

"I hated that place I'm Not Going back to that place" Luminita says

"It Will be a different school and it will be fun this time I promise"
Alice says taking

Another sip of her drink.

The waiter comes back by and lays two white cloth women's swim
suits on the table

He keeps walking on and says "Here you go Alice" as he played the
swim suits on the table

Which where one piece the style of the day in black letters stilted
across the front of the bathing

Suit in black letters are the name of the hotel Alice lays some money
on the table more

Than enough and stands up with her glass in her hand

"Let's go For a Swim "Alice says

Luminita stands up taking a sip from her Glass

Alice grabs the white suits on the table and walks out of the restaurant Luminita follows

They Go to the Part of the Palace That Has the Pools... at this point in history only the

Smaller pools are heated which have custom made bricks that they heat up and insert into

The water keeping the water hot they enter the dressing room to change Alice has a Locker

In the dressing room that they put their clothes in they pick their glasses up that they had

Brought with them

Luminita sticks her foot in the water it's hot

They get into the pool and sit down in the water which comes up to their necks

Luminita takes the largest sip of the Rabbit blood that she had taken she had a half of a

Glass left she feels another massive rush run all over her body and she gets even higher

Becoming drunk off the blood

"Alice when I go to Collage" Luminita ask becoming very sleepy

"Mabey 150 years from now is a good time to be in collage" Alice says

Luminita smiles and ask "How do you know Alice it will be good time in 150 years from now"

"It will be you can take night classes the world will have changed into a different place

And you will enjoy it the world always changes" Alice says Trying to cover up how she

Knew what the future would be like which was easy do to as Luminita had taken another

Giant drink from her glass she had one more large drink left she begins to drift off into

A euphoria she had never experienced before her body is tingling all over Alice's Voice

Is in her head but she hasn't a clue to what she's saying at this point Luminita has become

Addicted to this Rabbit Blood she will come back here to this place many times some of

Them without Alice for this Rabbit blood for as long as they have it Alice takes her glass

From her noticing that she has drank too much to fast Alice pours what's left into her own

Glass and sits Luminita down and her own glass down she brushes the hair back from

Luminita face "Sit up your going under the water" Alice says helping Luminita to

Sit up in the pool. Luminita Would Become A Powerful Killing Machine One Day

But Would Always Stay Loyal To Alice

Alice takes another rather large drink from her glass and then sits her glass down for the

Time being

Alice Shakes Luminita "Wake Up" She Says To the Drunk Vampire

"Come on Luminita let's get you home can you picture yourself standing at my fire I,LL get our clothes "Alice Says

Luminita responds "Ok Alice I'm standing at the fire "Luminita says standing in front of

Fire soaking wet she's having visions A Effect from the Rabbit Blood Alice Gets Out of the

Pool grabbing her glass leaving Lumina's empty glass siting by the pool she pours the rest of the

Blood in her glass in the garbage can and sits her empty glass down goes into the dressing room and gets their clothes

Out of the locker she vanishishes out of the room out of the palace
out of Budapest

And appears in Front of her fireplace in her home in Transylvania
    Luminita Bathing suit

Lay on the floor in front of the fire Luminita Was No Where to be seen

Alice Appears outside Lumina's Bedroom Door She looks inside Lumina's
Asleep Knocked

Out By the Potent Blood Alice Vanishes out Of the Room and BACK by The
Fire she picks the

Wet bathing suit up LAYS IT across the hearth takes the wet bathing suit off
her is wearing strengths it out across

The hearth she vanishishes and appears in her own bedroom light flickers as
the flames burn in

The torches on the side of the wall she hangs the close in her hands up in her
closet gets her bed

Robe on and goes to her desk the lamp is still burning she never lets them run
out of fuel

She sits down at her desk at Writes in her Journal She writes for about an hour then vanishes out

Of her room back to the fire and puts some wood that was stored by the fire into the fire to

Keep it going she looks at the master clock which is huge Its 5:45 Am Werewolf's was Almost

Extinct on Earth There Were only one in the forest of Transylvania And A Few Scattered

Throughout Romania in 300 years the moon had gotten just a short distance from planet earth

And by 1875 the werewolf's now only change during the first full moon of every month

Which is tonight Alice has been spending all of her full moons at the palace recently she and Luminita had been at tonight

She knew there was a werewolf in the forest she intends on staying up until surmise to make

Sure Lamina doesn't go to the forest in the middle of her euphoria which will keep her

Asleep for hours after dark but Alice stays up until the sun begins to peak over the

Mountains out her bedroom window she closes the curtains and gets into bed pushing the

Drapes clear Alice thinks to herself she forgot to show Luminita the safe room tonight says

To herself that she will show her in the next few days Alice falls asleep About 6:48am at this very

Moment the moon is still in the sky in these early hours and at this very moment at the

Home in the forest the one where Alice and Luminita Left the Deer a Werewolf Stood

Drinking some of the Blood That's Left in the Deer's Neck the Old Women has just gotten out of bed

She is going outside to get some firewood she opens the door The Werewolf Springs onto

Her Leaping from All Fours It Devours the old women and then goes into the corner and

Lays down and goes to sleep once the moon had went down it had transformed back into

The human form a girl not many years older than Luminita lay sleeping she awakes at 8:07AM

She saw what she had done and runs off crying into the forest Alice will either save

This girl or destroy her it all depends on how they meet and how honest the conversion is if

They have one at all if she meets her while she's a werewolf she will most likely have to

 Kill her but Alice's Blood Could Give This Girl a Real Chance Who Is Fighting this Desperately

She's doing the same thing Alice did she's hiding her clothes before she transforms and

Knows her way back to them even only changing once a month is such a traumatic

Experience that it's still rough and just as painful This Girls name was Rosemary she was

25 and was from Wallachia She Had Been on a Camping Trip to the forest of Transylvania With Her

Friends none of them believed in werewolf's or vampires and they thought it would be fun

To camp in the forest of Transylvania so they had made the trip one weekend the next

Friday Rosemary's friends were dead and Rosemary was infected by a werewolf because the

Group at planned their trip to purposely go on the full moon which was that Friday the

Werewolf was killed later that day by a werewolf hunter in the forest no one knows of

Rosemary she got all of the money that her friends had on them and what money she had

And she had been staying of all places in Alice's old Room At the tavern the room is still

Cheap and Rosemary is nowhere close to running out of Money she doesn't want to go home

Like the way she is afraid she will kill someone she loves she didn't know what was going

On at first she finally realized she was a werewolf when she turned into one she knew she

Had a wound from a werewolf claw and she got a room to see if she would turn into a

Werewolf on the next full moon and she did she's a waitress in the Traven she really doesn't

Need the money but it keeps her mind off of home and what she's dealing with Rosemary

Desperately needs some of Alice's or another Vampire that is old as Alice's she desperately

Needs some of this Vampire blood which way she will try and get it either as a werewolf

Or as Rosemary will be left on chance it all depends on how they meet Alice AS even seen

This girl working in the tavern but thinks nothing of her Rosemary was very smart

She already spoke English very well she went to a good school in the city. But she is

Missing she never told her family where they was going or that they was even going

She makes it Back to Transylvania she goes to her room and goes to sleep our story

Picks up a month later Feb the Third 1875 The Night of the next full moon The Night

Rosemary Meets Alice. Alice will have the power to save her or destroy her that will be a

Decision Alice Makes On The Spot........................

Feb 3 1875 6:59PM in the forest not far from Transylvania

Alice Had Awoken the MO moment the sun had went down
Luminita was still asleep

She had Made Alice Take Her back to Budapest to the palace hotel
for more Rabbit blood

As usually Luminita Had Abused the Potent Blood and Was
Sleeping it Off Alice had

Appeared In The forest after a walk around the Growing Village
streets the hour of

Light that was left the wishing hour as Alice had come to call it
.Alice was just up the

Mountain side from the old cemetery that she first awoke from some
300 years ago

She had just fed on some animal blood four young rabbits which had
a rather

Sweet taste and somewhat potent it was Alice's Favorite Animal
Blood and Rather

Hard to Get Alice Would Have to Appear as Fog she would watch the area As This Fog and for a Rabbit To

Come Out Of Its Den and She Would Appear With Her Hands on the Rabbit Which

Would Have a Powerful Bite for an animal that only eats greens she would just stretch

Their neck tight and when her Fangs would sink in the blood would literally spurt out like

Fountain Alice would drain the small animal in under 30 seconds she would usually drink

From about four of them when she could find them funny enough Luminita would

Someday even become addicted to this rabbit blood in the future

Which has turned Luminita into a Vampire version of a drug Addict which was not

Uncommon with young Vampires if the Vampire was on its own in this state of being

Addicted to potent blood they will surely draw too much attrition and the Young Vampire

Would Be Destroyed This Would Never Happen To Luminita As Alice Would Always

Be Around Her or Close By

Alice was walking around the Side of the Mountain She Had Some

Mountain Flowers She Was Headed for the Crave She Robed 300 Years Ago It's Dark

She comes Around a Small Hill and Runs Right into a Young Women They Bump Right

Into each other Alice Did Not Hear This Young Women Coming She Was Startled To

Walk Into a Human in the Forest without a Light

"Suttee bine".."Are You Ok" Alice Ask the Girl in Romanian

"Da, sunt bine trebuie sa plec Îmi pare rău pentru mersul pe jos in tine"...."Yes Am Fine I Must Be Going I'm Sorry for Walking into You" The Attractive Girl Says in Romanian

Alice Could See Her Face Very Well This Girl Worked In the Tavern Alice Thinks Her

Name Is Rosemary . "Așteaptă Tu nu ar trebui să fie în pădure seara nu e sigur și de ce nu ai o lumină cu tine"......."Wait You Should Not Be In The Forest Tonight It's Not Safe And Why Don't You Have a Light With You" Alice Frost says in the local Language

"Ai uitat Light Plec ar trebui de asemenea"......"Forgot Light i am leaving you should too" Rosemary says in her native tong

"Te voi merge pe jos acasa va fi mai sigur"....."I will walk you home it will be safer" Alice says in Romanian

Rosemary shakes her head and says " Nu am de gând acasa i-au să fie singur i-au pentru a merge"..."am not going home i have to be alone I have to go"

Rosemary walks on by Alice frost who didn't say anything else and just watched the girl walk by her

And watched her walk over the hill Alice was curious to this girl and the situation that she

Had met her. Alice Appeared over the hill as fog behind the girl about twenty feet she didn't

Suspect this girl of being a werewolf she was following her because she was concerned

About her she follows the girl about 15 mins as fog Alice Knows the Full Moon Will Be

Out in only a min or two Rosemary Stops and Looks in Every Direction She Sees Alice As

Fog but Rosemary as No Clue .The Fog Bank is Motionless. Rosemary Starts To Undress

"What The Hell" Alice's Spirit Says To Itself Silently

Rosemary Is Completely Nude She Hides her clothes in a bush in forest floor on the ground

At This Point Alice Frost Knows What This Girl Is and what's About to Happen

The moon reveals itself behind the Trees and Rosemary Falls to Her Knees and Screams

In Pain she begins to transform into a werewolf within 30 seconds she is a fully

Transformed werewolf howling at the newly risen full moon The Wolf Runs

Up The Mountain Side at High Speed At Times on All Fours It Disappears

Going over the other side of the mountain

The Fog Bank Turns into Alice Frost .She Stands unarmed and thinks for a few moments

She says to herself "I will confront Rosemary Tomorrow night at the tavern I think she gets

Off work at 8:00 PM I Will Offer To Help Her"

Alice vanishes from the spot in the forest that she was standing in and appeared in her

Own room Luminita was laying on Alice's bed she was waiting on Alice they was Going

To Budapest Again

. Alice ask Luminita How She Is Feeling

"Am Ready to Go Alice" Luminita says In a Unhappy Tone

Alice and Luminita Was Already dressed for their Trip

"I'm Ready Lets Go "Alice Says Walking Out Of the Room and into the room with the

Wall safe she gets a handful of the gold coins which was accepted at most locations in Budapest

She had about what was in today's money would be around 100 thousand dollars in both of her

Hands she puts the coins in the side pockets of her jacket she vanished and appeared back in

Room Luminita was standing waiting on her

"Appear in the same spot Luminita" Alice says

Luminita disappears

Alice vanishes and appears in Budapest at the back of the palace in some bushes Luminita is in

Them waiting on her. The Two Walk out from the bushes and enter the palace hotel from the rear

In a door that was left open for them by the waiter they walk down a hallway and past the pools

And back to the restaurant part of the hotel they are seated at their usual table .Rafael the same

Waiter Comes To Their Table

"The Same Tonight Alice" Rafael Says In A Friendly Manner

"Only Fill Our Glass Half Full Tonight Rafael" Alice Says

"Ok Alice" Rafael Says walking to a back room

Luminita turns her head and looks at Alice with her mouth open shocked that she was only going

To get a half of a glass of this potent heroin like substance

"Alice why only half Glass" Luminita says in a low voice

"I want you coherent Tonight Luminita I Have to Talk to You about Something" Alice says sharply

"Alice What Is Coherent" Luminita Ask beginning to be Satisfied Now with Only A half a Glass

"Luminita when you drink this blood you see things and you hear things your abusesing it

 You've

Become addicted to it your body craves it you're not in your right mind when you drink it" Alice says

Luminita does not say anything for a few moments

Then sees Rafael coming out of the back room and says "Here comes"

Rafael sits two sparkling wine glasses down and pours them half full. The two have two

New bathing suits in the locker in the dressing room they intend on going for another

Swim with their drinks. Rafael leaves the table

Luminita picks her glass up and drinks a large sip and lets out a deep breath this was a

New

Bottle and from a was most potent to Luminita

Luminita stands up with her glass

"Let's go swimming Alice" Luminita says looking at Alice

Alice stands up and the Two Vampires walk out of the restaurant which had about 50

People dining they walk back down the hall   toward the Pools

"What you want to talk about Alice" Luminita ask expecting it to be more talk of how she

Was addicted to Rabbit Blood but was surprised at what she heard

"Luminita we may be having a house guest soon it will be one person they will know we

Are a Vampire I Will Even Be Turning Them into a Vampire" Alice says as the two

Vampires walk down and go inside the dressing room

"Who Is It Alice" Luminita ask surprised

"Her Name Is Rosemary" Alice says stepping into the hot water of the same pool that had

Been heated and had fresh water in it

Luminita steps in the pool and sits down beside Alice

"Who is This Girl Alice" Luminita ask staring straight forward ahead of her into
Nothing

"This Girl Is in Trouble and needs help" Alice explains

"She poor like I was" Luminita ask in a brighter tone

"No that's not her problem she is a werewolf" Alice says

"Alice she will kill us" Luminita Says in a hyper tone after finishing her drink she sit the

Empty glass down on the edge of the pool

"No She is friendly I have talked with her briefly if she Accepts being a Vampire Which

She Probably Will the Werewolf Virus in Her will die and she will be a Vampire" Alice

Says in a teaching tone to her voice

"How long she stay with us" Luminita ask softly and feeling very high but not to the point

Where she is out of her head

"Just till her is on her feet as A Vampire I'm Planning on giving her 500 thousand American in gold she will be able to live where she wants" Alice says

"Why you do this for her Alice" Luminita turning looking toward Alice waving her

Hands back and forth in the hot water

"Because I've been in her situation before" Alice says revealing to Luminita the information that she was once a werewolf

"You Alice was werewolf" Luminita ask curiously

"Yep" Alice Says She still has almost all of her blood left in her glass taking another sip

"What was like Alice" Luminita ask

"Hurts Like hell" Alice says pouring a little of the blood in Luminita's empty Glass from her cup

Luminita picks the glass up and drinks half of what was in it

"You Think she has killed yet Alice" Luminita ask swimming out about four feet from Alice

"It's Hard to Say There was attacks recently the Old Women that we left the deer for was

Killed but if there was one werewolf in Transylvania Then There at one Time Been At Lest

Two so it could have been another wolf either way I'm going to help her" Alice says finishing her

Drink she swims to the other end of the small heated pool

Luminita finishes the potent Rabbit Blood That Alice Had Gave Her Swims to the side Alice

Is sitting at now and sits the empty glass down on the brick ledge

Luminita is the most stunning Looking Vampire of the Day with Her Eyes and beautiful

Red hair,

"Let Us Go Home Then" Luminita says

Alice swims in the middle of the heated pool they are the only two in the large open

Room with several small heated pools and a much larger deeper pool that was not heated

"In A While Luminita I'm Swimming" Alice says

They swim for a few mins more and Alice says

"Want another small drink Luminita" Alice ask

"Well let's get the drink then" Luminita says satisfied

The two Vampires Vanish from the pool and appear soaking wet in front of their locker

In the dressing room they grab two towels drying their hair. They undress and dry off

These are two of the beautifullest women in Romania your eyes are blessed if you see them

Nude dressing into their clothes. They sit down on the bench and finish dressing putting their

Boots on Luminita's boot has a higher hill on it but it came all the way to her knees and was skin

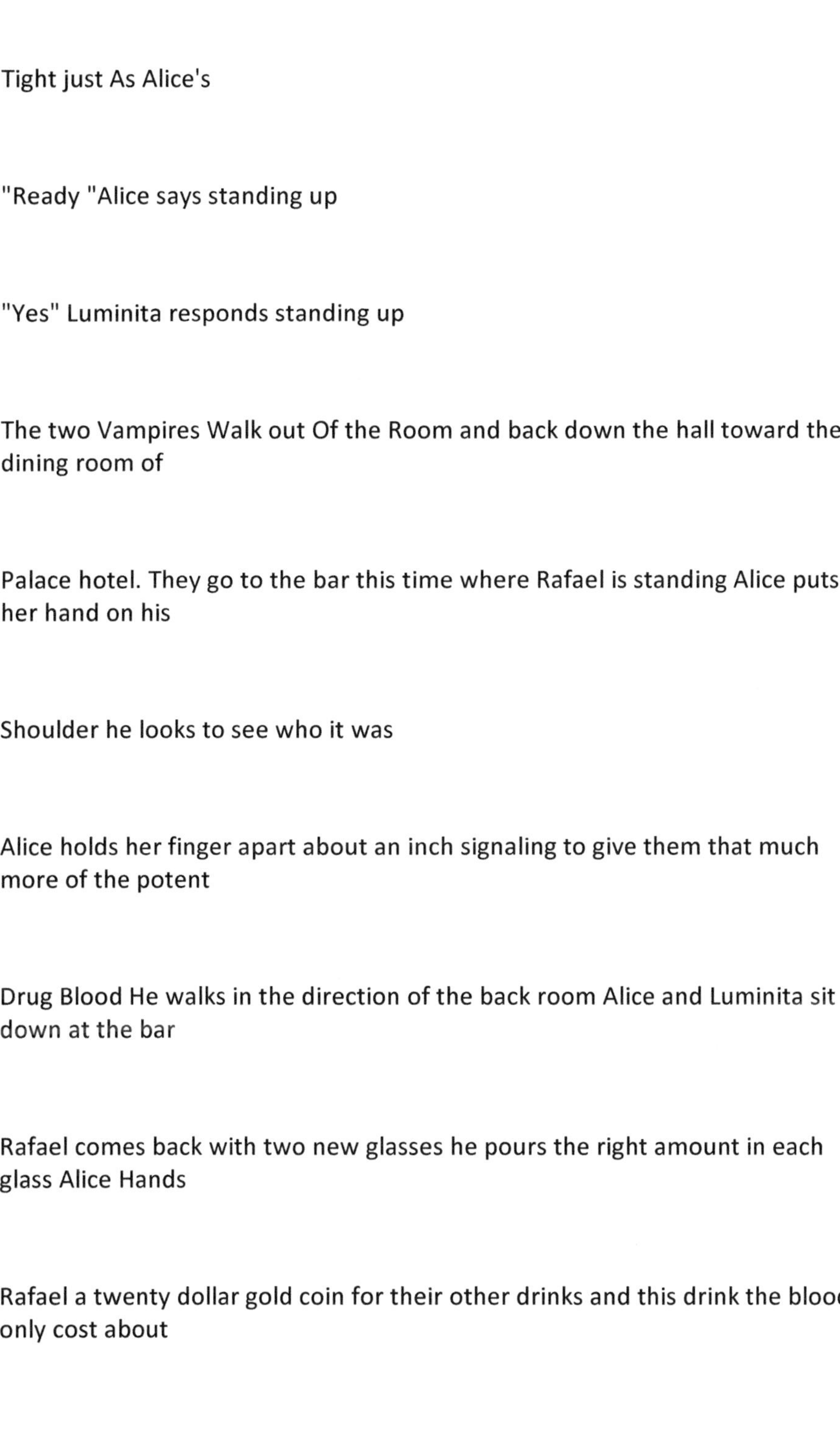

Tight just As Alice's

"Ready "Alice says standing up

"Yes" Luminita responds standing up

The two Vampires Walk out Of the Room and back down the hall toward the dining room of

Palace hotel. They go to the bar this time where Rafael is standing Alice puts her hand on his

Shoulder he looks to see who it was

Alice holds her finger apart about an inch signaling to give them that much more of the potent

Drug Blood He walks in the direction of the back room Alice and Luminita sit down at the bar

Rafael comes back with two new glasses he pours the right amount in each glass Alice Hands

Rafael a twenty dollar gold coin for their other drinks and this drink the blood only cost about

1.00 A glass and the rest of the money was a tip for Rafael he thank Alice and walked away

Luminita takes moderate size drink trying to not drink too much. A Massive rush the high really kicked in in both Vampires they didn't even get

A half a glass this time. Alice takes a sip and looks at Luminita who is finishing her glass as Alice

Looks at her Alice sees that she's had enough that the amount she drank tonight was her dose

And that's what she needed to drink every time and Alice judges in her glass which she just

'

Emptied into her mouth .she takes someone's drink that was left behind and pours an amount

 In her glass measuring the amount of this Vampire Drug to Let Luminita Consume the Next

Time They Came Here Which Would probably Have to be tomorrow night .Luminita looks At Alice

"Alice You going to drink that Alcohol?" Luminita Ask feeling warm all over she's as happy as she's

Ever been in her life. "I'm Just Playing" Alice Says Not telling Luminita the truth

.The two Vampires leave their seats and walk out of

The dining area and out the front doors of the palace it's still early on 1:09 Am.

Come Luminita I know another Vampire in the city he operates or well he has his servants operate

An expensive jeweler store in the city he will be up I'll buy You Something Come on" Alice says

Pulling Luminita by the arm

The two Vampires walk for about 20 mins and they come to the Shop there's A Light on inside

Alice knocks on the door. A Man that appeared to be about 40 years old comes and opens the

Door AND ASK FOR Alice and her guest to come in a friendly tone to his voice

"I Thought I Might Buy Something from You" Alice says to the Vampire Who is an older being than what he appeared to be

"I have many new items since you was last here just look around let know what you would like"

The vampire says to the two Vampire women

"Pick anything you want Luminita" Alice says

Luminita starts to look through the glass cases at all the necklaces and rings Luminita looked at

The

Prices the cheapest thing she saw was something that came to an amount in today's money that

Would have been 50,000 thousand American dollars she sees a ring that is price about ten

Thousand dollars more than that she likes it has a large diamond in the center and red large

Red ruby's set around the diamond Alice walks over to her

"Find Anything" Alice Ask

Luminita Points to the ring

"That's pretty it will match your necklace that what you want?" Alice ask

"Yes want that one "Luminita says shyly feeling ashamed at how expensive it was

Alice tells the other Vampire that they would take that ring Alice pays him in gold

It took most of the coins she had in her pocket. The Vampire hands the box with the ring

In it to Alice she hands it to Luminita she takes it and says "Thanks" she opens the box she

Takes the ring out of the box and try's it on it's a perfect fit she keeps looking at it as they walk

Out of the door of the shop they go back onto the street of Budapest it's empty

"Let's go home Luminita" Alice says

The two Vampires disappear from the streets and reappear in front of the fire place in Alice's

Home in Transylvania Luminita hugs Alice and says "Thanks again for present"

"We've both had a lot to drink let's just get some sleep I want you to act your best

When our quest arrives tomorrow night" Alice says

"Will be good" Luminita says

"Goodnight Luminita do not leave the house "Alice says

Alice vanishes

"Goodnight Alice" Luminita Says looking at her ring again

Feb 4 7:45 Pm 1875 Transylvania

Alice had slept late from drinking the potent blood the night before she gets out

Of bed and dresses in her black robe with the hood she vanishes and appears in some bushes

Behind the tavern she walks around to the door and goes inside and sits down at a table in

Back she looks for Rosemary who is serving and old man at a table a meal and drink Alice

Watches Rosemary for the next 15 mins while she worked there was a lot of people in the place

And Rosemary had not spotted Alice Watching Her Another waitress had waited on Alice who

Had ordered some alcohol just for looks she didn't drink any of it. 8:00 pm Rolls around and

The bar keep orders every one to finish up they will be closing in five mins.Every one

Finishes up what they are eating or drinking and people are getting out of their seats

Leaving into the streets of Transylvania which was blanketed with snow and it was still

Snowing. Alice stays in her seat for a few more moments then rises and slowly walks over

to Rosemary who is clearing a table

"Bună ziua Rosemary"..."Hello Rosemary" Alice Says in Romanian in a Low Voice

Rosemary Recognizes Alice the moment she looks into her face she looked worried when she

Saw Alice

"Buna ziua" ..."Hello" Rosemary says in Romanian in the same low voce that Alice Gave

Alice leans forward and whispers in Rosemary's ear and says "Știu ce sunt eu vă poate ajuta să Există undeva putem vorbi"..."I Know what you are I Can Help You Is There somewhere we can talk"

Rosemary has a shocked look on her face

"Putem merge în camera mea"...."We Can go to my room" Rosemary says in the same low voice

The two walks up the same set of stairs Alice walked up 300 years ago she shakes her head

As they come to Alice's old room and go inside Rosemary turns the knob up on the oil burning

Lamp and the room fills with more light

"cine ester tu"..."who are you" Rosemary says in a louder voice now still in Romanian

"Numele meu Este Alice Frost Sunt Original din America de"...My Name is Alice Frost I'm originally from America" Alice says a little louder in Romanian

"I Speak English" Rosemary says in an accent

"That's convent" Alice says

"You Can Not Help Me I'm cursed" Rosemary says in thick Romanian accent

'I Know you're a werewolf Rosemary I followed you last night I saw you transform I know what your

Going through "Alice says

"Crazy lucky you are not dead" Rosemary says not even realizing what Alice is

"Rosemary I'm A Vampire I can remove the curse of being a werewolf" Alice explains

Rosemary at first does not believe she is a vampire but Alice pulls her lips up and show Rosemary

Her fangs. Rosemary becomes frightened

"Do not be afraid Rosemary I will not harm you" Alice Says

"How can take curse away" Rosemary ask

"I will bite you will become a Vampire" Alice Says

Rosemary Looks uneasy And Says "And become another monster"

"Rosemary you're the monster I live mostly on the blood of animals as A Vampire you will have a

Life and you will be able to control yourself no more innocent will die from your hands" Alice says

Rosemary sits down on her bed

She stares off in the distance and says "Ok Alice bite me"

"Not here get your things we will inform the owners of the tavern you will no longer be working

Here

I can't quit my job I might need the money someday" Rosemary says

"Rosemary I Will Give you 500 thousand American in gold when you get on your feet as a vampire

Can live anywhere you want to in the world" Alice says

"Why you do this for me?" Rosemary ask looking into Alice's eyes

"If literally been where you are standing now some 300 years ago I was a werewolf just like

You I got my hands on some Vampire blood that as of yet is the only cure for the curse" Alice says

Rosemary's face was amazed that she was looking at a 300 year old vampire if she knew the

Whole truth of Alice and werewolf's and vampires her mind would really be blown .she gets off

Her bed and goes to her closet and starts putting her clothes into the bag that she had brought

Them camping in she gets them all and informs Alice she is ready she says her goodbyes as she

Leaves the tavern for the last time her and Alice walk the streets of Transylvania They make it

To Alice's place in under 15 mines Alice knocks on the Locked door Luminita hears the knock from

Her room she appears in front of the door and Ask who it is

"It's Alice Luminita" Alice says

Luminita unlocks the door and opens it the werewolf and Vampire have snow on their

Shoulders they come inside Luminita close and Locks the door behind them

"Rosemary this is Luminita, Luminita this is Rosemary I hope the two of you will be good friends" Alice says

"Hello" Luminita says friendly

"Hello Luminita" Rosemary says noticing The Eyes of the red headed vampire

Rosemary sits her bag in a chair and looks at Alice and says

"Let's get this over with" Rosemary says

"Follow me Rosemary bring your bag I'll take you to your new room "Alice says

Alice takes Rosemary up the stairs to the upper balcony and leads her to the room

One door down from her own room Luminita stayed in the master room by the fire

The Two Immortal beings walk into the room the torches shined brightly on the

Walls. Alice opens the closet door

"You can put your clothes in here there's already some of my clothes in it you can wear

Anything that will fit you" Alice says

Rosemary and Alice was exactly the same size

Alice walks over to Rosemary standing very close to her

"Are you ready" Alice Ask

"Will it hurt" Rosemary ask nervously

"Allot less than turning into a werewolf "Alice replies leaning in closer to Rosemary's neck

"I"LL Be Genital" Alice whispers softly inserting her Vans into Rosemary's Neck

Rosemary made a little notices but remain mostly quiet

The Tats Of her Blood which was sweeter than sugar

And just as potent as Rabbit Blood Alice had drank

Rosemary doesn't bleed as bad As Luminita Had Did When'

Alice had bit her

Rosemary feels dizzy from loosening the amount of blood she lost Alice had drank more from

Her than she had from Luminita

Alice keeps her from falling backward

"We Need to close your Wounds Rosemary let's see if Luminita Wants to go with us" Alice Says

Looking into Rosemary's vampire eyes

The Newly Born Vampire follows her 300 year old Creator out of the door they walk

Back to the lower level and Alice Ask Luminita If She Wants to Come with Them

"Yes Do" Luminita says

Luminita Vanishes

Alice Looks into Rosemary's eyes and says "Keep looking into my eyes"

Rosemary does and the room starts to spin she closes her eyes and her head drifts back a little and

She vanishes from Alice Sight

Alice Vanishes and Appears in the middle of the forest standing next to the two new Vampires

That had just vanished from her sight

Rosemary stood looking at the forest with her new set of eyes

"Wait here both of you" Alice Says in A Low Voice

Alice vanishes over the hill Luminita and Rosemary hear Alice Catch a Deer

Alice Pops Back In front Of the Two New Vampires holding a large female deer it is bleating

Loud Rosemary is holding her hands over her ears to keep them from hurting

Alice pulls the hair out of the deer's neck

"Come Rosemary Drink there could be more werewolf's in the forest" Alice says

Rosemary kneels down to the animals neck and puts her mouth on the deer and her fangs

Go into the animal with ease

Her eyes widen when the blood enters her mouth the deer gives a final blade and dies as most

Of its blood had been drained Alice stops Rosemary and tells her that's enough she looks at her

Neck the wounds healed Rosemary was now a Healthy young Vampire

Alice explains to her how to travel and Rosemary Vanishes From the forest and appears

Back in front of Alice's fire place she feels like she has never felt before the deer blood

To Rosemary was as potent as any blood she stands tingling all over with

Powerful flushes of energy surging all over her body Alice and Luminita appear next

To her at the fire

"You feel this way every time you drink blood" Rosemary Ask Alice

"Yes different blood is different levels of potency with rabbit blood being the

Strongest Luminita has a little problem with it "Alice Says

"Rabbits" Rosemary says

"Yep rabbits have that most potent blood of any animal" Alice says

It Was Now 4:06 Am Alice Puts the Young Vampire That Had Just Fed to Bed
.She returns

To the forest in a different location and feeds herself for the night she
appears back

In her room gets into her bed robes writes a little bit in her journal and is in
bed By 5:35 Am

Her last thoughts before she goes to sleep are maybe take them to Budapest
tomorrow

Time Trip Chapter Seven 2024

Budapest 8:45 Pm inside Alice's home in Budapest the year is 2024

Alice Why Must Go to Collage Now I didn't go when you like you said this will probably be

A terrible time to be in Collage besides I have learned all I need to know in school from you

And as a Vampire I don't need collage" Luminita says As the Three Vampires stand in the master

Room of the Budapest home which was just as large as her home a Transylvania which

Had not been lived in in 100 years Alice appears there in the home every three or

Four months to make sure everything is still there she has taken the contents of the safe

With her to Budapest but there is still many fine paintings and all kinds of valuable

Swords suits of armor and everything that was originally in the home remained Alice's

Bag of gold coins it was a rather large duffle bag was worth an estimated 207 million

Dollars by this time Rosemary had stayed with Alice and Luminita all these years

"Come Luminita will be fun" Rosemary says to Luminita as she was going to be going with

Her. "This is an even better time to go to college Luminita I checked it out" Alice says

Sipping from a wine glass Luminita had over 350 rabbits in the basement in cages Alice had

Made her draw some blood from each of them and store the blood in containers so she could take it with her to

Collage Alice Has picked the school that they are going to they are going to Berkley and it

Cost a rather large sum of money to get them in as they had no school records they all had

Fake IDs now in these 149 years Luminita has become pretty smart learning many

Languages and has read many books in many different subjects

Why Must we go to Berkley Alice" Luminita says who had given Alice Allot of problems over the

Last 149 years

"It's a good school I checked" Alice says

Alice Still Wore Allot of Her Old Clothes but Luminita and Rosemary dressed in modern

Goth Clothes a Fade That Had Risen in the years past

The Three Vampires Had Already Vested the Collage One Early morning while it was

 The right time of the day to appear there Alice Had Taken Each Vampire there one then

 Going back getting the other one because they had never been there .This was the

Collage that Alice Had Went to Infect the Human version Of Alice Frost has been born

She is 19 years old and will be attending Berkley for 4 years Alice Frost the Vampire intends

On Letting Luminita and Rosemary Go to the same school she's going to and See if they

Meet and what happens Alice intends on telling the two over a 100 year old vampires

The truth when they ask her by telephone about the girl that looks just like her but younger

And has her name it will be an interesting conversion .They are both already packed both

Of them have oversize camping backpacks carrying bottles of rabbit blood Alice signed them

Up to a few Classes that she knew she would be in to get them started they had picked the

Rest of their classes the right time comes for them to travel there Alice goes with them

It's the wishing hour here in an hour the sun will be up Rosemary and Luminita Will be

Staying together in the same room it will just be them in the room the room has been

Prepared for them by someone Alice got to Black the windows out it's on the third

Floor no one will break in on them in the middle of the day while they sleep and

No sunlight could enter Alice even had better thicker windows put in Case some

Kid Luminita pisses off throws a rock at their window in the middle of the day

The Three Vampires Pop into being at Berkley behind the main building in some

Bushes they start to head for their dorm each of the girls carry bags even Alice

They make it to their room they go in and close the door behind them

There's three beds but they will be the only ones in the room it was arranged that way

By Alice when she donated the 10 million dollars to the school which had agreed to

Allow the girls to attend no questions ask the 19 year old Alice the human has

Some night classes with The Two vampires She Will Even Sit behind the Two Vampires

The Three Vampires Say Their Goodbyes Alice tells them to stay out of trouble looking

At Luminita as she said it and tells them each to not turn anybody into a vampire while

They are there They Agree and Hug Alice And then Alice Vanishes Back to her home

In Budapest. THE two vampires stand Alone in their room they take their backpacks

Off and each pull out a bottle of rabbit blood which they plan on getting high off of and

Going to sleep for the day as they are normally up and active in Budapest The two

Vampires Both Take Huge drinks from the bottles within 10 mines they curl up

On their bed and fall asleep they awake at 6:45 PM they both have a night

Class at 7:00 pm it's one of the classes Alice the Vampire picks out for them the subject included all things

That dealt with space and exploration of space Luminita was not looking forward to this class

The Vampires Arrive 1 Min Late to the class the teacher was not there yet students

Walk through the door and find a seat. Luminita and Rosemary are seated close to the back

Next to each other Luminta's Mouth hangs wide open in shock and curiosity when she sees

The young human 19 year old Alice Frost walk in the class she stares at her as Alice walks right by her

And sits down in the seat behind her Luminita turns around and looks at her again

She turns back around and tells Rosemary to look at the girl sitting behind her. Rosemary's

Mouth hangs open too you can almost see her fangs

"She as to be an ancestor of Alice" Rosemary says To Luminita

"Talk to her" Luminita says

Rosemary turns around and says "Hi My Names Rosemary This is Luminita"

"Hi My Names Alice it's nice to meet you two" The Younger Alice Says Very friendly

The Vampires Look At each other when she says her name is Alice

"That's a pretty name what's your last name" Luminita ask her in a friendly voice

"It's Frost" Alice says

Luminita Mouth hangs wide open when she hears her last name her fangs are exposed

Alice Notices them and says "Oh did you get your teeth caped"

Luminita closes her Mouth quickly and says "yes I did, who was you named after

Alice" Luminita ask

Alice smiles at Luminita and Says "My Grandmother"

"Where are you Two From" Alice says opening her book

We are originally from Romania I was born in Transylvania we have lived in Budapest for years" Luminita says

"Wow Transylvania I have Always loved the Vampire Stories" Alice says

"YOU like Vampires?" Luminita Ask Looking over to see Rosemary's face

"Yes I have always thought that the vampire stories are really cool" Alice says noticing

Luminita Vampire eyes

.

"Hey you want to come to our room later tonight and study" Luminita ask her hoping

She will say yes

"Sure I have one more class after this and I'm done for the day I can make it in abbot an hour

And a half will you still be up then" Alice says smiling At Luminita

"Will be up all night" Luminita says happily

"When do you sleep" Alice ask

"Sleep during day" Luminita says in her Transylvanian accent

"You sound Cool when you talk I like your accent you even sound and look like a Vampire"

Alice says.

The teacher

Comes in the room and class begins. Before the Class is over Luminita Talks to Alice

Before they Leave Camila Stands next to them quietly

Luminita gives Alice their room number and the three go there on way for the next hour

And a half

The two vampires go back to their dorm they only had one class their first night there

"But it's Not Alice Its More than like an ancestors of hers" Luminita say

"Ok will find out about her" Rosemary says

An hour passes by

Knock at the door each vampire grabs their bottle of blood that they had out and take the biggest

Drink they could get down and then put the bottles back up in the bags they came in

"That's her you get the door Rosemary" Luminita says

Rosemary opens the door and Alice says hello

"Come in Alice" Rosemary says

Alice comes in carrying books she sits them down on the desk in the room

"Hi Luminita hi Rosemary" Alice says

The Vampires look at each other then look back at Alice

"Let's sit down and talk" Luminita says

Alice sit between the two immortals on the bed she is the only one that has a book in her

Hand. Alice reads to them a while from the book about their next lesson in the night

Class that they have with each other. Luminita looks at Rosemary with a bored look on her face

"How long have you two known each other" Alice says

"For A While now" Luminita finally speaks

The three study for several hours' time passes fast for them Alice says I think it's time to go to bed now I'll see you two in class tomorrow" Alice says

"Want to do again tomorrow night" Luminita ask

"Sure I need to study has much has I can" Alice says

Both the Vampires look at each other

Alice grabs her books and says she will see them tomorrow night in class

"Will walk you to your room" Luminita says

"Will be right back Rosemary" Luminita

And Rosemary stays and gets into bed drinking

 By the time Luminita had got back Rosemary had drank some more blood
and fallen asleep

Luminita had stay at Alice's for about an hour and talked some more

Alice was expecting her roommate. Luminita goes back to her

Room and slips into bed and falls asleep with in mints

.......Luminita looks at this Younger Alice As her dearest friend she will watch
out for her at school she tells herself in her sleep

This human Alice who will go on her mission in a few years in the future the moment

The human Alice is invested by the werewolf on the ship the Alice who was a vampire

Would vanish from the year 2058 she would wake up back in her spot by the cemetery back

In the year 1575 as a werewolf she has all her memories of her life as a vampire and she

Takes care of the problem this time quickly knowing what to do and say. Alice has reached

A new type of immorality she is on continuous repeat of her life every time back to

The year 2058.Luminita takes it hard when Alice disappears and she has no clue in 2058

What happened to Alice and almost goes crazy looking for Alice .100 years later in 2158

The then brilliant vampire throws herself in her work the vampire has a breakthrough and

Develops a time travel devise at which point Luminita uses the technology to travel back in time

Where she can stay for three days at a time continues her relationship with both Alice

The Vampire and Alice the human .Tomorrow

Luminita will call Alice the vampire in Budapest and will learn the truth about the human Alice

And where werewolf's and vampires come from she will be shocked and almost can't believe

But does tomorrows a Friday she will ask the human Alice to study again

At 6:25pm the next night Luminita and Rosemary awake early during the wishing hour

Luminita Grabs Her Phone which she had called hand held talking device when

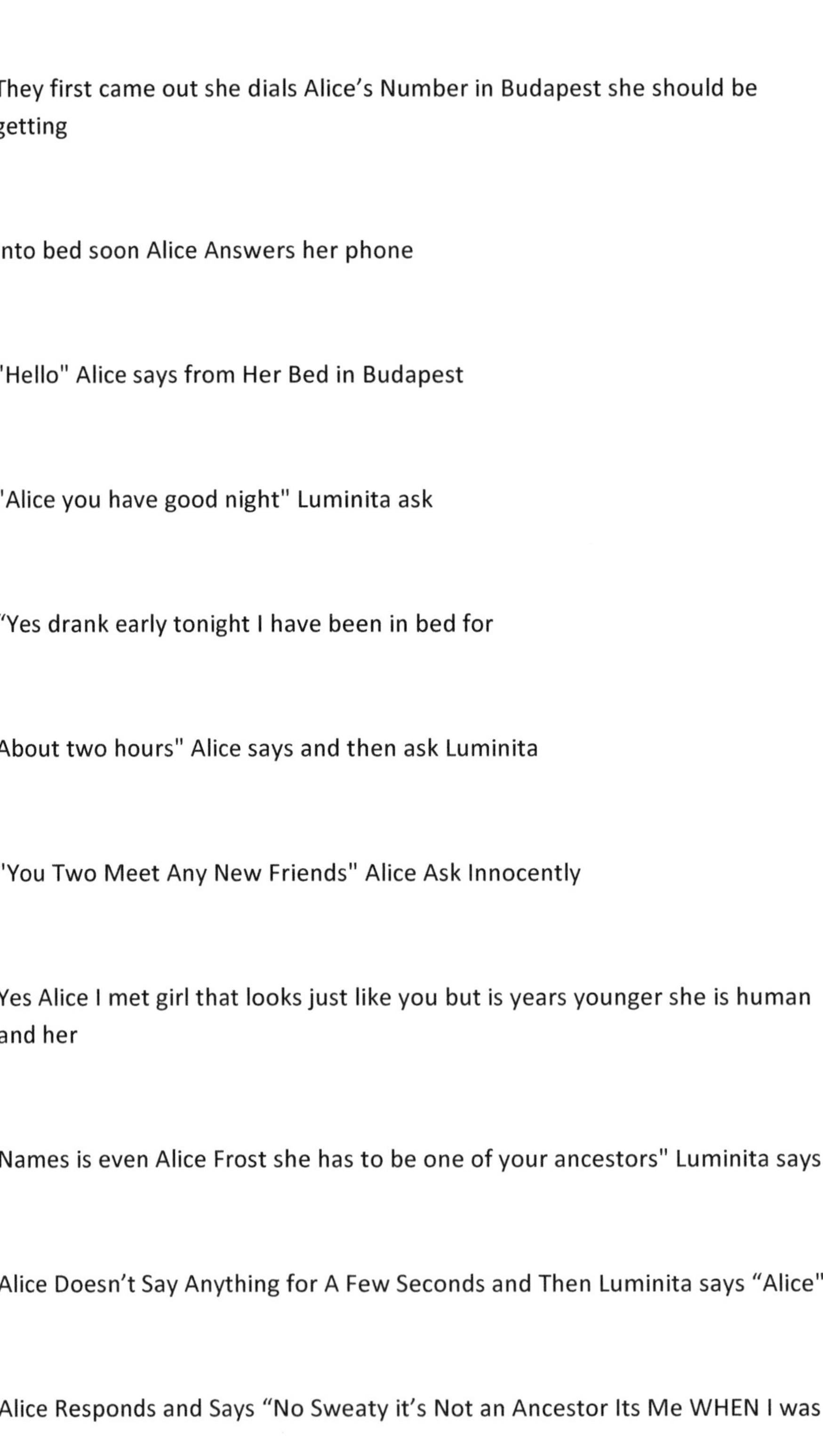

They first came out she dials Alice's Number in Budapest she should be getting

Into bed soon Alice Answers her phone

"Hello" Alice says from Her Bed in Budapest

"Alice you have good night" Luminita ask

"Yes drank early tonight I have been in bed for

About two hours" Alice says and then ask Luminita

"You Two Meet Any New Friends" Alice Ask Innocently

Yes Alice I met girl that looks just like you but is years younger she is human and her

Names is even Alice Frost she has to be one of your ancestors" Luminita says

Alice Doesn't Say Anything for A Few Seconds and Then Luminita says "Alice"

Alice Responds and Says "No Sweaty it's Not an Ancestor Its Me WHEN I was a human

Alice explains her whole story from start to finish Telling Luminita the Truth About

Werewolf's And Vampires and about Were They Had Originated From

"You Kid me Alice" Luminita says expecting Alice to say she is joking and that it is in

Fact an ancestor of hers living now But Alice Says

"No Joke it all happened" Alice says

"This is unreal" Luminita says finally knowing the truth of what she and her new family

Was.

"Luminita listen to me this is very important don't discourage this younger version of

Me from reaching her dreams of going into space one day because if she doesn't go

None of us will exist" Alice says in a teaching tone

"Understand Alice will not discourage" Luminita says still in disbelieve

"And Luminita do not turn this new Alice into a Vampire even if she finds out your

A vampire and begs for it do not do it" Alice instructs Luminita

"Understand Alice Will Not" Luminita says   as Alice tells her she is drifting off to sleep

That she needs to go on To Class.

Luminita tells Alice the vampire Goodnight and Hangs the phone up Rosemary had been standing

In front of her the whole Time trying to find out what Luminita was so shocked

About which she knew had something to do with this new girl that looked like Alice

And even had her name. Luminita explains the whole ten min conversation

She had just had with Alice. Rosemary was still saying "I can't believe it" As
The two

Walk to their first Class of the night which was the same class they had met
the

Younger Alice   the Two Vampires enter the class room this times right at
7:00pm

They spot The Younger Alice in the Same Seat Rosemary was wearing more
Goth

Clothes but Luminita had put on an Outfit that was Very unusual it was an
outfit

That had Belong to Alice Frost Some 300 Years Ago it still looked in good
shape

Luminita picked it from her closet in her room knowing It Would Attract the
Younger

Alice Who marveled at it when she saw The 300 year old wardrobe

"OH God Luminita I Love What You Are Wearing" The younger Alice says

"I know you Like Alice" Luminita says with a different tone to her voice

"I've Never seen clothes like these were did you buy it at" Alice the human ask as she opens

Up the jacket and gets a better look at the shirt Luminita has on

"These very Old clothes Alice They Belong to an Ancestor of Mine It Was Made

By A Fine seamstress in Transylvania   some 300 years ago" Luminita says siting in the

Seat in Front Of the Young Human Alice Frost

"God It Still looks in style and it's in such good shape to be that old" Alice says to her

"This was best money could buy at the time Alice that's why it's in such good shape" Luminita says

Alice opens her book and starts to read the chapter they are about to study

"You come over again tonight Alice" Luminita ask her

"Yes but it will be a hour later I have to help a friend with a subject" Alice says glancing up

From her book smiling at Luminita then looking back down at the subject she was reading

 Alice looks up to Notice Luminita Fangs Alice had Leaned Forward and Pulled Luminita Lips up

To Get a Better Look at Them

"You Stay longer tonight Alice" Luminita ask

"I Have No Classes Tomorrow Sure I Can Stay. You Know Luminita you're going to meet

A Nice Guy Someday and Fall In love And He will make you get rid of these teeth of yours" Alice Says To Luminita Letting go her Lips

Rosemary was not even listening to them

Alice Smiles with Her Pen Touching Her Lips She Looks Back

At The Subject she was reading the class begins and is over in an hour. The Two Vampires

And The Human Alice Get out Of Their Seats and start walking out of class Alice is in

Between the two of them. Alice Says" I'll Be over in A Couple of Hours" To the Two

Vampires Alice walks on her way and the Two Vampires go to their next class

"It's ok Rosemary it's just Alice if she finds out we are vampires its ok" Luminita says not thinking anything

About it As She said it

Rosemary Does Not Respond Any More right now but before they get to their next class

She looks At Luminita and says "I Do Not like This Luminita. You Can Do It But it makes

Me unhappy" Rosemary says going into the class leaving Luminita Standing at the Door

Luminita does not know any better she thinks it will be ok if this Alice finds out they are Vampires

This Young Alice Frost One That she intends on studying Again Tonight hopefully

.The two Vampires finish all their class they have for tonight and go

Back to their room. In two hours The Younger Human Alice will arrive. Rosemary Gets

A bottle of blood from her bag she sits down by Luminita takes a big drink and hands her

The bottle Luminita takes a larger drink wishing she could let Alice try some of the blood

With it having the same effects on her

Rosemary shook her head a little bit and took another large drink of the potent blood

Which gave both the Vampires a massive rush of energy

 Rosemary Grabs the bottle from her and drinks for as long as she can

And Says" I'm going to Sleep Luminita Have fun" She says laying down in the bed

Across the room turning toward the wall

"You No want to study Rosemary?" Luminita ask in a soft tone to her voice

"No Have drank too much have fun" Rosemary says and is asleep within five mines

By the time Alice knocks on the door later than the night Rosemary was passed

Out and in a dead Vampire sleep .The Two Vampires Still had for them what a human would call

Jet lag they surely was asleep in Budapest at this hour. Luminita opens the door and waves

For Alice the human to come in she has books with her this time and she had changed into shorts

And a different shirt

"Like clothes Alice" Luminita says as Alice walks in the door

"Just Something Comfortable" Alice says

"What's wrong with Rosemary" Alice ask

"Oh She Drank Too Much She Will not be studying with us tonight" Luminita says

..The Two Girls study and talk until 4:00 am in the morning

But none of it wakes Rosemary Up. Alice and Luminita Eventually fall asleep in the floor

Alice stays The Whole Night and sleeps part of the day there

Alice awakes the next night at 6:05 pm.

"What time is it" Alice

"Is 6:05 Pm" Luminita says

"Dam We slept all day" Alice says looking over at Rosemary in the other bed who was still

Asleep.

"You Leavening Alice?" Luminita ask

"I Thought We Might All Three of us go get some food tonight maybe drink a little" Alice Says

Luminita Face Changed Expression

"Am Not Hungry Alice but Will Go with You" Luminita says

"Are you old enough to buy Alcohol   Luminita" Alice Ask as She Watches the Red Headed

Vampire Get Dressed

"Am only 19 but have fake ID" Luminita says

 Who is now fully dressed in the same clothes she had on last night the ones Alice had liked

"Well let's wake Rosemary and go" Alice says

"Rosemary Always sleep late when she drinks too much she will be asleep for few hours more"

Alice didn't have any Jeweler on She didn't even have her ears pierced

Alice Notices the Ring That Luminita Has on It's the same one that she would buy for

Luminita in 1875 in the Shop in Budapest

"Oh Man that's a beautiful ring Luminita" Alice says admiring the ring

Luminita takes the ring off and says "Here Alice You Have"

Alice Looks shocked and says" No I couldn't it Looks Expensive"

The ring had been valued a couple of years ago by an insurance company. They valued

It at 1.4 Million dollars

"Is Expensive Alice I Have Many nice things I want you to have it" Luminita says Handing Alice

The Ring. She Takes It Still shaking her head and says" I Have some Money Saved Up

Luminita I'll Buy It from you what's it value?" Alice ask Luminita

"Is Worth 1.4 Million Dollars Alice I Have Many Others" Luminita Says Taking the ring and

Slipping it onto Alice's Finger and Says "I Want You to Have"

"Luminita I Can't take a ring from you that's worth over a million dollars" Alice says taking it

Off of her finger

Luminita puts the ring back on Alice's Finger And says" Family Very Rich Would mean

More to me if you take"

Alice Looks at the Ring the Large Diamond Surrounded by Equally large Ruby's the ring

Band was made from 24 K Gold

Alice Hugs Luminita and say the same words that Luminita said to her when she originally

Bought it for her" Thanks For the Present"

"I'll Return It to You Someday" Alice says still admiring it

Alice Would Give the Ring Back To Luminita in 1875 As She Now Had the Ring with Her

On Her Trip to Space

Come Alice Lets Go Feed You and I'll Buy You Drink" Luminita says

The Two Walk out the Door closeting it softly to not wake Rosemary

There was 47 mines of day light left it was wishing hour here as Luminita had heard Alice the vampire

Call it before the two walk to Alice car it was a nice sports car a graduation present

From A Lady Overseas that had Known Alice's Family Alice had never met the women

But she talked to her on the phone and told her thank you the women sounded very

Young on the phone she was supposed to be very old

The two pull into a restaurant that Alice had been eating at ever since she arrived at the school

They Get Out Of the Car

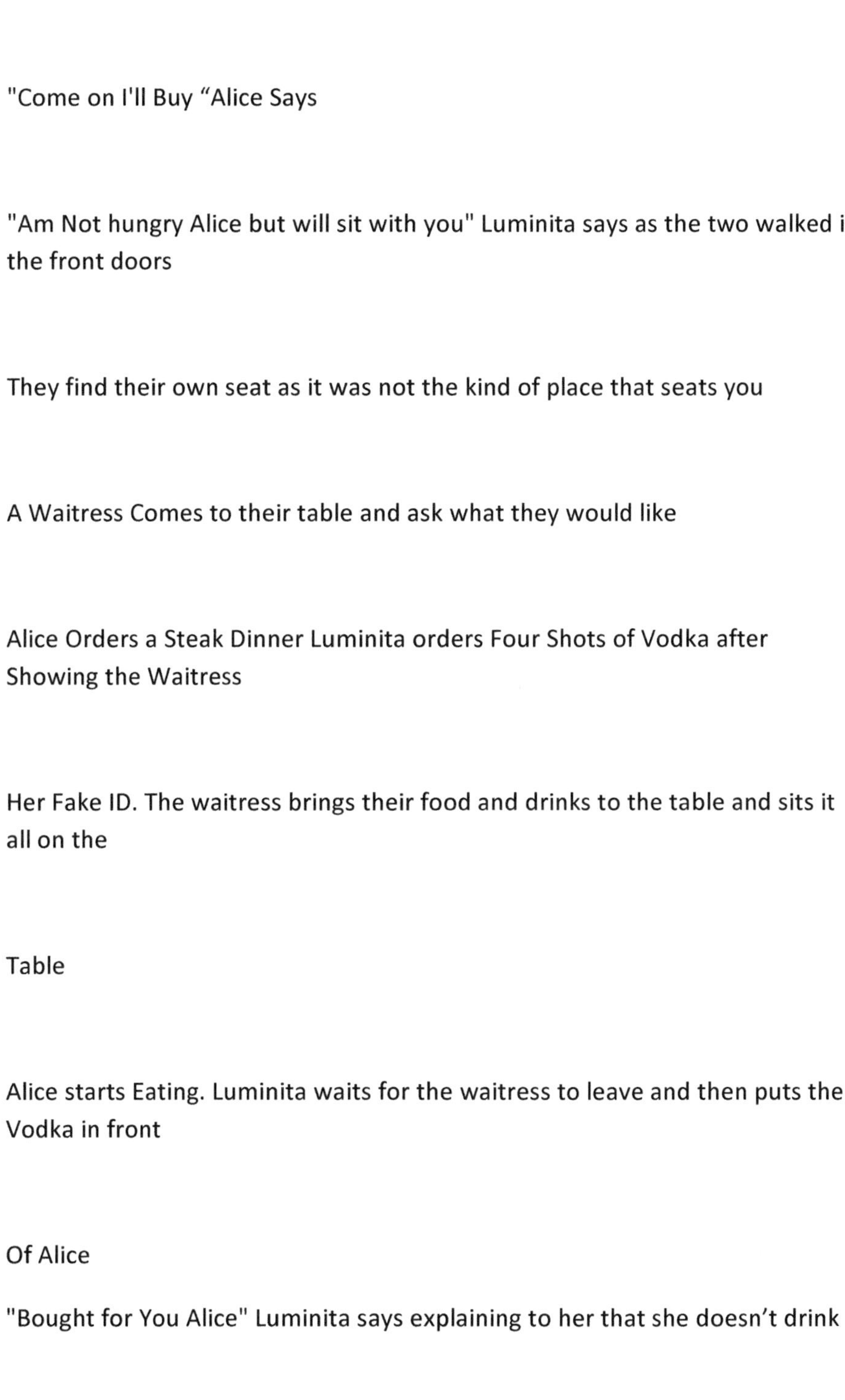

"Come on I'll Buy "Alice Says

"Am Not hungry Alice but will sit with you" Luminita says as the two walked in the front doors

They find their own seat as it was not the kind of place that seats you

A Waitress Comes to their table and ask what they would like

Alice Orders a Steak Dinner Luminita orders Four Shots of Vodka after Showing the Waitress

Her Fake ID. The waitress brings their food and drinks to the table and sits it all on the

Table

Alice starts Eating. Luminita waits for the waitress to leave and then puts the Vodka in front

Of Alice

"Bought for You Alice" Luminita says explaining to her that she doesn't drink

"Thanks how you knew I Liked Vodka" Alice Ask While Eating Fast

Alice the Vampire Had Tried To Drink Vodka in 1875 with Luminita Alice Had Cursed

When As a Vampire When She Threw the Vodka up Saying "Admit I Use to Love This Stuff"

"Lucky guess I Guess" Luminita says giving her no more information about the subject

Alice the Human Had Eaten Fast She Finished Most of the Steak She Cuts A Small

Piece of the steak stabbing the small piece with her fork she holds it to

Luminita Mouth and Says "Try A Bite They Have Good Food Here"

"Will make sick" Luminita says declining the small bite of human food it was dark out now

Alice Drinks Her Four Shots of Vodka one right after the other she lays some money

On the table Luminita says "I pay Alice" laying a 100 dollar bill on the table

"Thanks Luminita" Alice says standing to her feet a little wobbly

From the four shots of Vodka

Luminita Rises to Her Feet and Grabs Alice's Keys from Her Hand

"I Drive Alice" Luminita says

"You probably will have to I'm Already Drunk" Alice says laughing and snickering she brings

Her hand over her mouth to try and not be so loud

Luminita Had Never Met a Drunk Alice By the time Luminita had come to live

With Alice as A Vampire the Rabbit Blood Would Have A Different Kind of High Than

You Would Get from Drinking Vodka She had never seen Alice This Loose

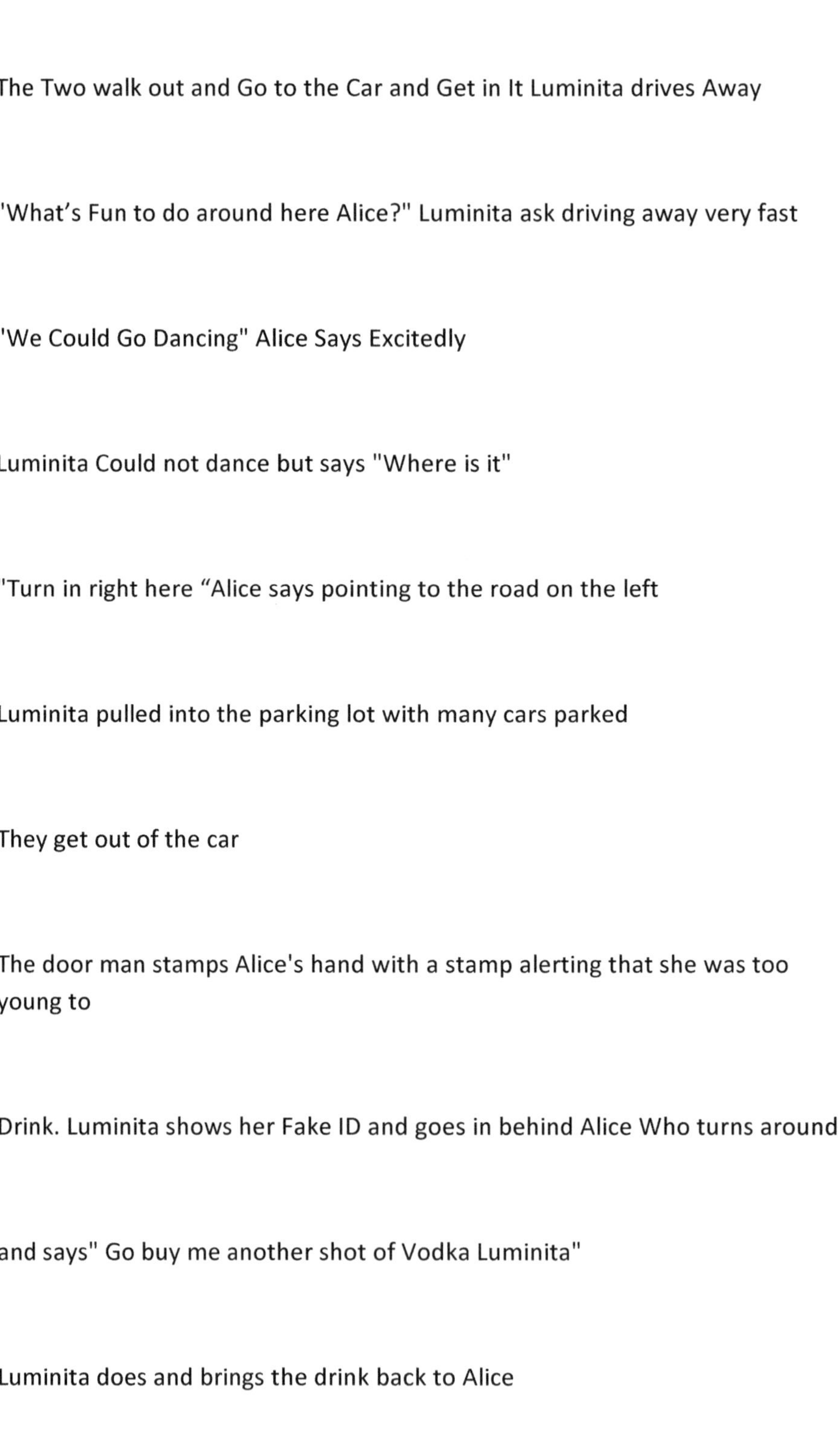

The Two walk out and Go to the Car and Get in It Luminita drives Away

"What's Fun to do around here Alice?" Luminita ask driving away very fast

"We Could Go Dancing" Alice Says Excitedly

Luminita Could not dance but says "Where is it"

"Turn in right here "Alice says pointing to the road on the left

Luminita pulled into the parking lot with many cars parked

They get out of the car

The door man stamps Alice's hand with a stamp alerting that she was too young to

Drink. Luminita shows her Fake ID and goes in behind Alice Who turns around

and says" Go buy me another shot of Vodka Luminita"

Luminita does and brings the drink back to Alice

Alice drinks it all down in one big drink

Alice was too drunk to dance now so they sit down at a table in the back

A waitress comes to their table she ask if they would like anything. Alice kicks Luminita

Under the table signaling her she wanted another shot of Vodka

"Bring me shot of Vodka "Luminita says showing the waitress she has no stamp on her hand

Alice doesn't say anything to the waitress who walks away from the table returning A

Few moments later siting a Taller shot of vodka than Alice had At the Restaurant

Luminita waits for the waitress to leave and she slides the shot to Alice who drank

It instantly Alice had drank six shots of vodka she would be deathly sick later

The two sit at the table for the next 20 mines talking then Alice Looks at Luminita and says

"I'm going to be sick" wobbling back and forth it was still early only 9:05pm

"Come Alice let's get some air" Luminita says helping the young human drunk Alice to her

Feet. Two walk outside where Alice bends over throwing up the meal she ate

And all the vodka she drank

"Oh My God Luminita I'm so sick I Think I'm dying" Alice Says vomiting stomach fluids now

Luminita Puts Her in the Car and Drives Off As Fast As She Pulled in

Alice Is So sick she can't even stick her head out the window to vomit she just bends

Over and throws up in floor of her car

"Oh My God Luminita I think I have alcohol poisoning take me to the ER Please" Alice says crying

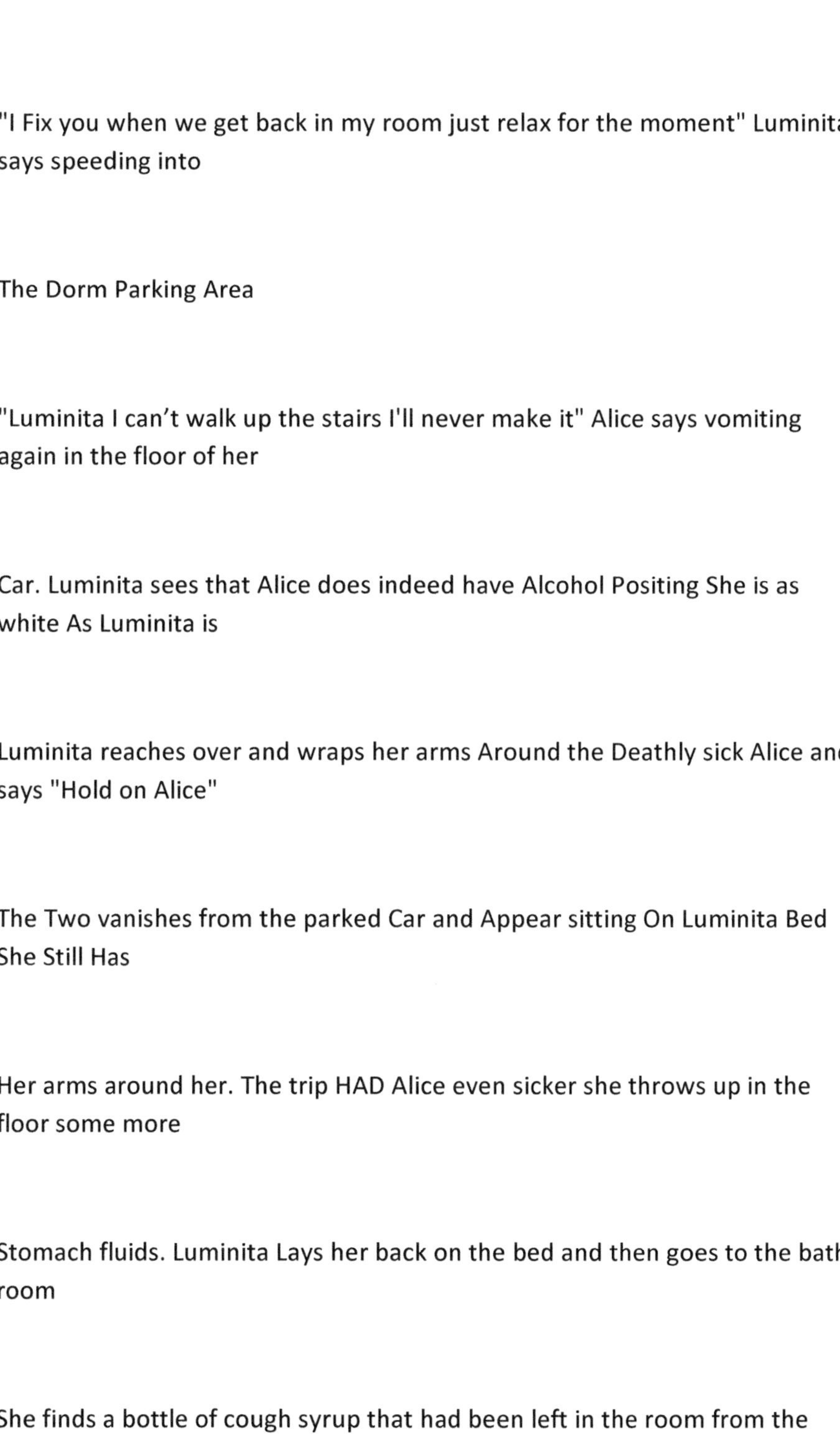

"I Fix you when we get back in my room just relax for the moment" Luminita says speeding into

The Dorm Parking Area

"Luminita I can't walk up the stairs I'll never make it" Alice says vomiting again in the floor of her

Car. Luminita sees that Alice does indeed have Alcohol Positing She is as white As Luminita is

Luminita reaches over and wraps her arms Around the Deathly sick Alice and says "Hold on Alice"

The Two vanishes from the parked Car and Appear sitting On Luminita Bed She Still Has

Her arms around her. The trip HAD Alice even sicker she throws up in the floor some more

Stomach fluids. Luminita Lays her back on the bed and then goes to the bath room

She finds a bottle of cough syrup that had been left in the room from the

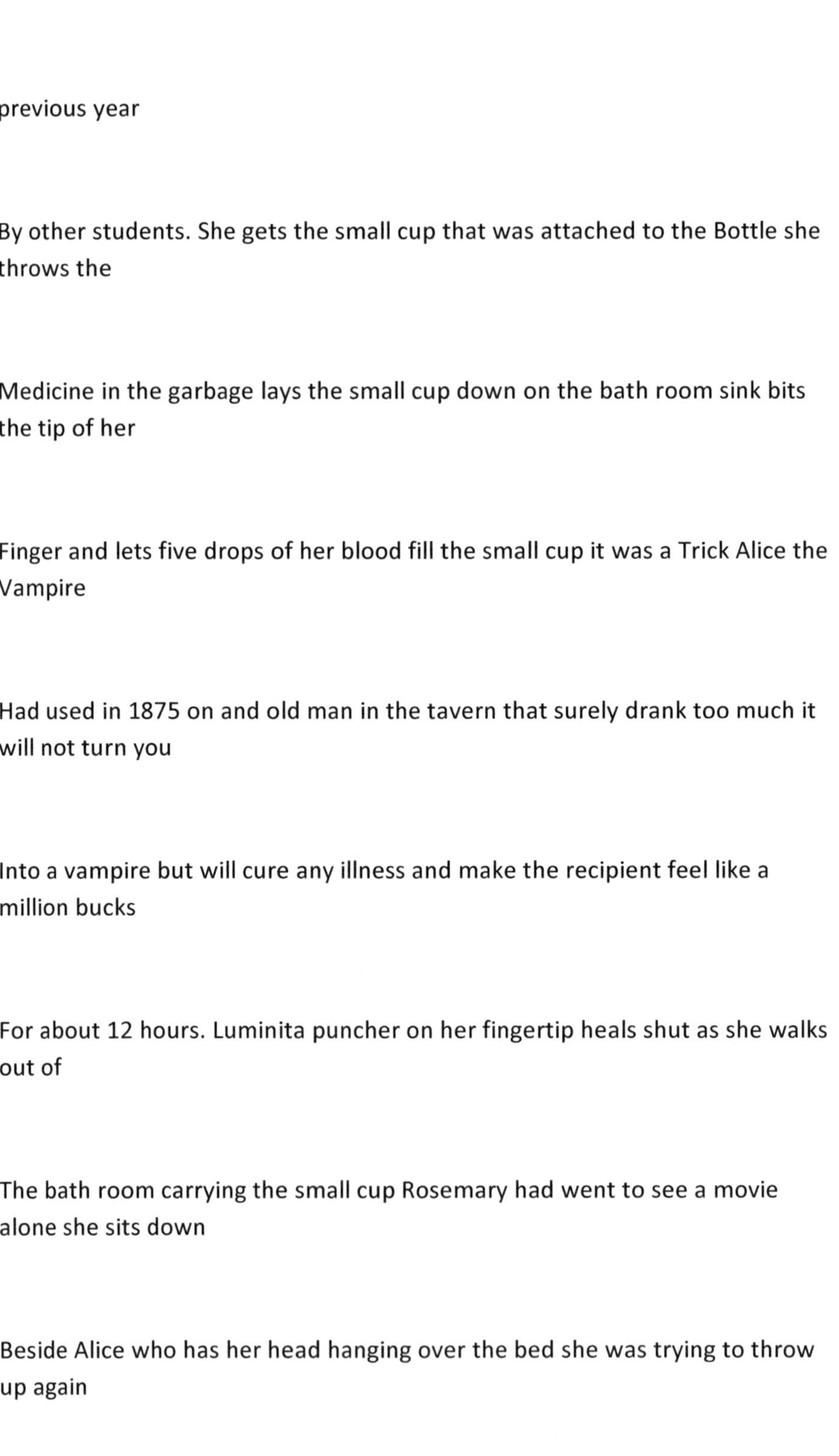

previous year

By other students. She gets the small cup that was attached to the Bottle she throws the

Medicine in the garbage lays the small cup down on the bath room sink bits the tip of her

Finger and lets five drops of her blood fill the small cup it was a Trick Alice the Vampire

Had used in 1875 on and old man in the tavern that surely drank too much it will not turn you

Into a vampire but will cure any illness and make the recipient feel like a million bucks

For about 12 hours. Luminita puncher on her fingertip heals shut as she walks out of

The bath room carrying the small cup Rosemary had went to see a movie alone she sits down

Beside Alice who has her head hanging over the bed she was trying to throw up again

But had threw up so much she could no longer produce any vomit

"Here Alice Drink this it will make you better" Luminita says raising Alice up in the bed

Who said? "How did we get in the room" to Luminita who said "I Carried you"

"What" Alice says dry heaving again trying to throw up?

Luminita opens Alice's Mouth and pours the blood down her throat. The Moment the Few

Morsels of blood reach her stomach her eyes get wider than Luminita had ever saw them

They turn to vampire eyes for about 20 seconds and then return to their natural color

Alice is fine now better than fine she does feel like a million bucks

she looks at Luminita and ask her" What was that I drank I want some more"

"You can't have anymore right now" Luminita says

"Is It an Illegal drug or prescription medication" Alice Ask sitting up with her feet touching

The floor now

"It is neither illegal nor prescription it was 5 drops of my blood" Luminita says feverously

"Blood" Alice says a little shocked

Luminita opens her mouth showing her Fangs again and says "Am Real life Vampire Alice"

Alice was feeling the effects from few drops of Luminita Blood which was really kicking

In she was high as a kite higher than she had ever been in her life she believed Luminita

"Oh My God" Alice says Pulling Luminita lips up to look at what she now knows is

Real Vampire Fangs. "How old are you" Alice Ask curiously

"As a Vampire I'm 149 years old I was 19 when I became a vampire in 1875"

"Thanks...For everything" Alice says softly

"Feel Better now" Luminita

"Yeah I Feel like a rock star" Alice says

"Luminita Make Me a Vampire" Alice Says Desperately

"Not right now Alice You will be A Vampire someday but not today

Alice looked like her heart just got broken

"Why Not Now" Alice says in a disappointing way

"A Vampire can't travel in space Alice" Luminita explains

"How did you know I was getting to go to space" Alice ask

"Know a lot about you Alice you will understand one day" Luminita says

Rosemary comes in the door it was about 3:57 Am she feels lonely

She drinks some rabbit blood and lays down on the bed

Alice goes back to her own room to get ready for class the next day. At this point

Alice is fascinated by what she now knows is two real life Vampires

IN the year 2158 the then brilliant vampire Luminita worked for the United States

Government on the time travel devise that Luminita develops by the year 2168 Luminita

Did many time jumps and unauthorized time experiments in her research she comes?

Up with a plan to get Alice the Vampire from being stuck in the past which she had vested

Many times And Alice the vampire was very proud of her achievements Luminita was an expert at time

Travel and its effects on the world she informs Alice the Vampire That She Is going time Jump

Back to the Year 2024 Bite the Human Alice and Turn Her Ion a Vampire Explain to Alice Of

The Past that when She Turns the 18 year old human Alice into a vampire that Alice would

Appear back in her Budapest home in the same spot she disappeared from she will come back

To the year 2058 that the events that take place on the mission to Gemini 1 have already

Happened once and was imprinted on their world and time and that's all that has to be done

The Vampire Alice tells her no that it could work out differently that it could destroy them all

But Luminita is confident in her research and goes ahead with the plan but as she was about to

Travel to the year 2024 top ranking people that was over the time travel project confronts

Luminita about all the unauthorized time jumps and the experiments she had been doing

They inform her that they are removing her from the project and that she will have nothing

Else to do with it .Luminita is upset but she knows her work is over in this lab. She goes

To her desk and grabs her pc Tablet which had all the designs and blue prints on it to

Construct the time travel devise she plans on building her own in Alice's old home

When the top ranking people see her with the tablet they try to stop her. They ask for the

Tablet she refuse to surrender it they try to take it from her. The vampire goes on a mad

Killing rage and kills everybody in the lab she vanished to Alice's Home in

Transylvania

And there constructs another time travel devise she had the only one she set the other one

In the lab to self-destruct. The lab was built into a mountain side it blew the top of the

Mountain off leaving a giant Hole in the top of the mountain if it had not been built

Into the mountain when the devise blew up it would have destroyed the city below

124 people died in the lab that night most from the explosion in 2178 Luminita

Constructs her new devise in her Transylvania home and finally carry's out her Plan

She Travels Back to Berkley in the year 2024 the Sunday night that Alice had went back to her

Room. She has a conversation with herself first and informs herself what is going to happen to

Alice In 2058 when she disappeared Luminita was amazed by the story she heard from herself

And agreed with herself they must try and save Alice.

Luminita of the future appears at Alice's Room she knocks on the door

Alice opens it she thinks it's the Luminita that she had just saw she Ask her to come in and

Luminita does.

"Alice I have changed my mind I am going to make you a vampire right now" Luminita says

. She wraps her arms around her and the two disappear

And reappear in the home in Budapest Luminita bites Alice

Alice's Color leaves from her face and her eyes turn to her new vampire eyes

Luminita gets a half a bottle of blood that was in the house and only pours

Alice almost a full glass a little over half full the new Vampire drinks the blood closing

The wounds on her neck at which point Alice the Vampire that was in the past reappears in the Budapest

Home a lives on past the year 2058 where there two Alice Frost One the Old vampire

And the newly created 19 year old Alice the Vampire the year is 2200 Both Alice's the old vampire and the 19 year old vampire and Luminita

And Rosemary Live in the same house together. The young Alice has been told that the women that

Looks just like her is her ancestor which was a decision made By Luminita knowing that it would

Be better if the younger Alice never knows the truth...